Tw...
One UNIFORMLY HOT! miniseries.

Don't miss Harlequin Blaze's first 12-book
continuity series, featuring irresistible soldiers
from all branches of the armed forces.

Watch for:

A FEW GOOD MEN by Tori Carrington
(Marines)
January 2009

ABLE-BODIED by Karen Foley
(Delta Force)
February 2009

ALWAYS READY by Joanne Rock
(The Coast Guard)
March 2009

THE RIGHT STUFF by Lori Wilde
(Medical Corps)
April 2009

AFTERBURN by Kira Sinclair
(Air Force)
May 2009

LETTERS FROM HOME by Rhonda Nelson
(Army Rangers)
June 2009

Uniformly Hot!
The Few. The Proud. The Sexy as Hell.

Blaze

Dear Reader,

When my editor asked if I'd like to write a story for the UNIFORMLY HOT! miniseries, how could I resist? After all, there's nothing more sexy than a man in uniform! But researching the day-to-day life of a Delta Force soldier proved to be challenging, to say the least. My persistent questions eventually attracted the attention of Big Brother, although I'm relieved to say their investigation didn't involve helicopters or men in black, wearing night-vision goggles, rappelling onto my roof. But just in case, I made sure I wore my cutest pajamas to bed each night!

The last thing Delta Force operator Ransom Bennett needs is a distraction, no matter how enticing. Sidelined by a combat injury, he knows his only mission is to prove to his commanding officer that he's able to return to duty, the sooner the better. He should be focused on getting well and getting ready for his next assignment, but all he can think about is his new neighbor Hannah Hartwell. And when Hannah tells him she can cure his injury with her unique, hands-on treatments, he finds even the most hardened of soldiers can sometimes have a weak spot....

I hope you enjoy reading Ransom and Hannah's story as much as I enjoyed writing it!

Hugs,

Karen

Able-Bodied

KAREN FOLEY

HARLEQUIN®

TORONTO • NEW YORK • LONDON
AMSTERDAM • PARIS • SYDNEY • HAMBURG
STOCKHOLM • ATHENS • TOKYO • MILAN • MADRID
PRAGUE • WARSAW • BUDAPEST • AUCKLAND

Recycling programs
for this product may
not exist in your area.

ISBN-13: 978-0-373-79455-3
ISBN-10:   0-373-79455-X

ABLE-BODIED

www.eHarlequin.com

Printed in U.S.A.

ABOUT THE AUTHOR

Karen Foley is an incurable romantic. When she's not working for the Department of Defense, she's writing sexy romances with strong military heroes and happy endings. She lives in Massachusetts with her husband and two daughters, and enjoys hearing from her readers. You can find out more about her by visiting www.karenefoley.com.

Books by Karen Foley

HARLEQUIN BLAZE

353—FLYBOY
422—OVERNIGHT SENSATION

Don't miss any of our special offers. Write to us at the following address for information on our newest releases.

Harlequin Reader Service
U.S.: 3010 Walden Ave., P.O. Box 1325, Buffalo, NY 14269
Canadian: P.O. Box 609, Fort Erie, Ont. L2A 5X3

Winston Churchill once said,
"We sleep soundly in our beds because rough men
stand ready in the night to visit violence
on those who would do us harm."

This book is dedicated to those men.
Thank you for your service.

Prologue

NED SULLIVAN STARED in disbelief at the man who stood in front of him, squirming like a rat caught on one of those rodent glue traps. Even the guy's eyes bulged as he swallowed hard a couple of times.

Disgusted with the other man's obvious fear, Sully turned and looked out the window of South Boston's 32nd Precinct, across Colombia Road and toward the harbor, where an enormous oil barge was slowly being towed in by a ridiculously small tug. He knew just what it was like to be led around by the nose by something so small and seemingly insignificant.

"Whaddya mean she's *gone?*" He kept his voice low, but only an idiot would mistake the menace in his tone, and Mick Mahoney was no idiot. The two men had gone to grade school together, and if anyone knew what it was like to get on Sully's wrong side, it was Mick.

"I mean the shop is empty."

"Empty? Whaddya mean, *empty?*"

"She took everything. Even that glass display case where you said you stashed the money. It's gone," he explained, his words tumbling over themselves.

Sully's hands tightened into fists at Mick's words. "You were supposed to be watching her."

"I was, Sully," Mick said, his voice insistent. "I swear it. I was parked right there on the corner all night, waiting for her to lock up and go home, but she must have been working late because the lights didn't go off. Then Maureen comes up to me, and you know she's got the sweetest little—"

"Maureen, as in Maureen Hurley?" Sully spun back toward the other man, interrupting him.

"Yeah."

Sully glanced quickly around them, unwilling for their conversation to be overheard by any of the other sergeants or lieutenants working at the precinct. When he turned back to Mick, it was all he could do not to wrap his hands around the other man's neck.

"You moron." His voice was deceptively soft. "That twit, Maureen, just happens to be Hannah's best friend. So while you were letting your *dick* do the thinking, Hannah got away."

Mick shook his head in denial. "No way. I know what you're implying and it ain't true—that girl was hot for me."

"*That girl* used the oldest trick in the book to distract you while *my* girl skipped town. What'd she do? Lure you into the backseat and beg you to go down on her?"

He knew from the way Mick's face reddened that he was right. He snorted in disgust. "Yeah, kinda hard to keep an eye on Hannah's apartment when your face is buried in pussy, ain't it? I hope it was good for you, 'cuz guaranteed you ain't gonna get a repeat offer. That was a one-time-only, blue-light special, my friend."

Mick glanced quickly around before leaning closer. "Oh, yeah, well, at least I got that. What'd you get? *Nothing.* Except a lot of shit from the boss, and that newspaper article you're so proud of."

He jerked his head in the direction of Sully's wall, where an assortment of commendations, citations and newspaper articles had been carefully framed and hung. In the center was an article whose bold headline stated, Shopkeeper Accused of Selling Sexual Healing. Beneath the caption was a photo of a pretty young woman in handcuffs, being led out of a small shop. The sign over the door front read Body & Soul—Spiritual Wellness & Healing. She looked shell-shocked.

"So you busted her," Mick hissed. "Big deal. Even you—the great Sergeant Sullivan—couldn't get the charges to stick. And now she's gone, and your money is gone with her. You'll probably never find her."

"You're kidding me, right?" Sully tapped one finger against the silver badge on his uniform shirtfront. "I got this, which means eventually I'll get *her*. There ain't no place she can run to that I can't find her. Besides, I got you and the boys to help me."

"Oh, yeah? So you find her. And then what?"

Sully smiled. "Then I get everything that little bitch owes me. Fifty thousand dollars and a piece of that sweet little ass she's been swinging in front of me for the past year. She'll find out there are consequences for refusing me and then running off with my money."

Mick snorted. "It's not like she even knows about the cash."

"Yeah, well, if you'd just grabbed it when you were in there, like we planned, I wouldn't be in this situation."

Mick glanced nervously over his shoulder. "Why'd you ditch it in her shop anyway?"

Sully felt his face tighten. "Things were getting hot. Both my partner and my wife were getting suspicious and I needed a safe place to keep the money, at least temporarily." He shot Mick one dark look. "I would have had it back more than two weeks ago if you hadn't screwed up."

"You told me to go in and get the money from that display case where you hid it," Mick said, "but *she* came out of the back room and caught me snooping around. She thought I was there for one of her energy treatments. What was I supposed to do? I let her give me a treatment." He paused in recollection. "I'm telling you…it was like she could actually *feel* the pain I have from that old shoulder injury. She put her hands there, and it was like freaking magic. The pain vanished, just disappeared."

Sully smirked. "What a crock of shit. All she did was distract you from getting my money out of that cabinet."

"Oh, yeah? Well, Cronin says that dough belongs to him." Mick's fear visibly decreased a little when he spoke of Craig Cronin, an influential Boston businessman, and the undisputed top rung of organized crime in the Northeast.

Cronin's influence extended from Maine down to Florida, and only a few people knew how deeply entrenched he was with both the local and state police. Supported by political corruption on one side, and a deadly alliance with the Irish mob on the other, he was untouchable. He was involved in racketeering and extortion, and who knew how many people he'd made disappear. But his close affiliation with the top brass meant he'd never spend a day in jail. Mick probably felt a little inviolate himself, since Cronin was sleeping with Mick's sister. Nobody messed with Craig Cronin, not if they wanted to live.

Mick glanced around to ensure they couldn't be overheard. "If you don't get that money back, he'll make sure you get busted down to patrolman. You'll be pulling Code Nineteens for the rest of your career. You better find her."

"Oh, I'll find her, all right," Sully said, smiling grimly as he envisioned Hannah Hartwell's shock when he showed up on her doorstep. "There was never any doubt about that."

1

HEAT LICKED at her skin, made her shift restlessly and moan softly in distress. Her breath came in soft pants. She was hot, feverish with need. The man's hands moved over her body, touching and stroking her in all the right places. His mouth trailed moistly along the length of her neck and he took her earlobe between his teeth and bit gently, then soothed the sensitized flesh with the tip of his tongue.

She wanted desperately to see his face, but with his lips working magic along the whorl of her ear, she couldn't focus properly. He moved over her, his shoulders impossibly wide. She stroked her hands along the long, firm muscles of his back, and lower. She cupped his lean buttocks, loving how they flexed beneath her fingers, loving how he drove forcefully into her, pushing her higher and higher. Her thighs clenched around his slim hips, striving for the release that was so close. The inner muscles of her sex gripped him, reveling in his size and power. He stroked her, filled her, the rough silk of his flesh demanding a response. With a soft cry, she arched against him, rubbing her breasts against his chest. She was so close….

His movements quickened, became stronger. Her fingers fisted themselves in the sheets as the force of his thrusts caused the headboard behind her to thunk against the wall. Faster now, harder…if she could just see his face, look into his eyes…her climax was so close now.

Thunk, thunk, thunk.

The headboard reverberated against the wall as he filled her, stretched her, pounded into her.

Thunk. Thunk. Thunk.

Oh, no, please no. She was losing the feeling, moving back from the brink of what promised to be an exquisite explosion of pleasure. The surge of intense sexual need was receding. Even the hard masculine heat stroking between her thighs was vanishing, leaving her with only a throbbing, unfulfilled ache, and the thunking of…what *was* that noise?

Slowly, Hannah Hartwell came awake, disoriented and very much alone, still clinging to the vestiges of the erotic dream she'd been immersed in. It had seemed so real. She could still feel the hard length of her dream lover as he'd plunged into her, still feel the moist sweep of his breath against her ear and the weight of him pressing her down into the bed.

The abrupt ending of the dream left her bereft. Maybe, if she closed her eyes tightly, she could go back. She knew if she were to touch herself, she'd be wet and swollen with desire. It would take no more than several quick strokes of her fingers to ease the throbbing ache that still tormented her. How long had it been since she'd had good sex? Too long.

Thunk. Thunk.

Rolling onto her side, Hannah groped for the bedside clock, peering at it through the darkness. Jeez. Two-thirty in the morning. God, it was hot. Even the fan whirring softly in her open window did little to ease the sticky heat that had gripped the region for the past week.

Flopping onto her back, she stared at the ceiling and listened to the sound of something hard and dull striking the floorboards overhead. What the hell were they doing up there? Without central air-conditioning, the building was oppressively warm. It was probably even worse in the apartment upstairs. While she understood how the heat could make sleeping uncomfortable, if not impossible, it wasn't an excuse for being disruptive.

She'd moved into the first-floor apartment just six days earlier, and had yet to get a full night's rest, thanks to whoever lived in the apartment above her own. Every night, at nearly the same time, she was awakened by the strange thumping noise. She was beyond exhausted. She didn't know how many more interrupted nights she could handle. If it wasn't her neighbor keeping her awake, it was her own vivid imagination.

Despite telling herself that Sully had no idea where she was and wouldn't come after her even if he did, she couldn't quite convince herself of that. She'd heard rumors that he was connected to the mob, although at the time she hadn't believed them. He was a police officer, after all, sworn to serve and protect. In the weeks following the break-in at her South Boston shop, he'd come around every day to check on her. She hadn't suspected that he had an ulterior motive until the day he'd tried to pressure her into having sex with him in the back room of her shop. She'd been shocked and insulted, knowing the officer had both a wife and kids at home.

She'd refused, of course, but her life had taken a downward spiral as a result. She still had nightmares about the day he'd arrested her in a petty attempt to get back at her for rejecting him.

She'd been acquitted of any wrongdoing, but she'd been too afraid of reprisals to stick around. She knew what Sully was capable of, and the knowledge terrified her. Even now, the slightest of noises made her jump. Several times, she'd caught herself glancing over her shoulder as if expecting to see him bearing down on her, his eyes filled with gleeful retribution.

She was safe. She just had to keep reminding herself of that.

She'd put eight hundred miles between herself and Sully. Cliftondale, North Carolina, was a far cry from South Boston, and while she missed the brownstones and cozy pubs of East

Broadway, and the eclectic mixture of Irish locals and the artsy college crowd who had patronized her little New Age shop, Hannah didn't miss the anxiety she'd lived with.

She'd actually encouraged Sully to come around, at least in the beginning. She'd sensed a conflict within him and had hoped to perform a Reiki treatment on him. Her intuition had told her that if anyone needed spiritual balancing, it was Sully. But she'd quickly learned he wanted more than energy healing. Hannah still couldn't believe she'd misread him so completely. But all that was behind her now. She was making a new start.

In conjunction with the tiny furnished apartment, she'd also leased the first-floor storefront of the quaint little clapboard building, hardly able to believe her luck in finding two perfect rentals available under one roof. For a summer resort town, the combined rent was incredibly affordable. The fact that Labor Day had passed and Cliftondale was heading into its off-season didn't deter Hannah at all. The shop was hers.

Her parents had tried to dissuade her from using her "gift," convinced that doing so would only bring her trouble. Hannah understood their reluctance; her aunt had also inherited the ability to feel and soothe the physical pain of others through the touch of her hands. Aunt Elle had joined a nationally televised faith-healing ministry and her healing abilities had become legendary. At least, until the day the founder and minister of the church was arrested for solicitation. Overnight, Aunt Elle was decried as a charlatan. She had returned to Boston to live with Hannah's parents, but the press had been relentless in hounding her. It had been more than a year before their lives had returned to normal, and Aunt Elle had had to give up her energy healing.

Which was why Hannah had chosen a more subtle venue in which to use her own healing abilities, because despite her parents' misgivings she couldn't deny her skills. Helping others was a physical imperative, a calling that she was unable to ignore. She was a master Reiki practitioner, and most of the time she restricted her treatments to just Reiki. But occasionally, if she sensed a client might benefit from her unique healing touch, she would use her skill to help ease a particularly painful joint or muscle.

The past week had been an endless cycle of moving furniture and boxes into both the apartment and the shop. Only ten days remained before the grand opening of her holistic health and wellness shop, and she had a laundry list of things to do before she could open the doors to the public.

Her muscles ached from the physical demands of moving, and she felt ill from a lack of sleep that no amount of meditation or yoga could restore. She knew the erotic dream she'd had was her body's way of releasing the stress and pent-up anxiety she subconsciously harbored, and now even that pleasure had been denied her.

Lingering frissons of sexual arousal still teased her, and Hannah briefly considered satisfying herself. In the same instant, there came another thunk on the ceiling overhead.

With a groan, she sat up and swung her legs to the floor. Perched on the edge of the bed, she scrubbed her hands over her face and then tucked her hair behind her ears, debating what to do. She could ignore the disturbance, bury her head beneath her pillows and hope to get at least a little more sleep. She could make herself a strong cup of coffee and tackle the unpacked boxes stacked throughout the apartment. Or, she could go upstairs right now and confront her neighbor. One thing was clear—she couldn't go on like this. Something had to be done, and since it seemed her neighbor was as wide-awake as she was, now was as good a time as any.

Determinedly, she made her way across the dark bedroom. A full moon streamed silver light through the windows and illuminated the storage boxes stacked haphazardly along the perimeter of the room. She'd get around to unpacking them eventually, but not until after her business was up and running.

Unlocking her apartment door, she peered cautiously into the shadowed hallway. The staircase that led to the second floor was dimly lit by an overhead light. From where she stood, she couldn't see the upstairs apartment door. She'd been curious about who lived there, but mostly in terms of whether they were strong enough and willing to help her shift her heavier pieces of furniture around her own apartment.

She'd spotted an old, black Land Rover parked in the narrow driveway alongside the house. Two mornings in a row, she'd been awakened early by the engine throbbing to life, but she hadn't been quick enough to catch a glimpse of the driver as the vehicle reversed out of the driveway. She was always plugged into her iPod when she worked in the shop, and hadn't heard the Land Rover return, or its owner climb the stairs to the second floor.

Twice, she'd crept partway up the staircase, intending to introduce herself, but each time the sight of the closed door had unnerved her. In the end, she'd decided against asking for help and had done the majority of the work herself.

She'd spent most of the past week in the shop and hadn't seen anyone enter or leave the building. Aside from the late-night thumping, there'd been no other sign of life from whoever occupied the second-floor apartment. There was no name on the mailbox secured just above hers beside the front door; nor had she seen any mail being delivered to it.

She'd even snooped around the building a little, stepping into the tiny backyard to stare up at the second-floor balcony. But the sliding doors had been closed, the curtains firmly drawn, and there was nothing on the balcony itself to indicate who might live there. No flowers, no table or chairs, no wind chimes, no nothing. In fact, if it weren't for the late-night disturbances and the Land Rover sitting in the driveway, she'd be convinced the apartment above her own was empty.

Glancing down at herself to make sure she was adequately

covered, Hannah decided her tank top and men's boxer shorts were more than conservative enough. The tiny coastal town of Cliftondale was an artists' haven, and during the hot summer months the narrow, winding streets swarmed with college students and tourists who wore less clothing than she did right now. She wasn't wearing a bra, but then she barely filled a B-cup, so it wasn't like she had a lot going on in that department to worry about.

It didn't matter. She was going upstairs, regardless.

Hannah drew in a deep breath, striving for a calm, serene manner. This wasn't a confrontation. It was an opportunity to make a new friend, to connect with another human being and extend herself. She had a natural gift for communing with others, and she had no reason to think this occasion would be any different.

She climbed the staircase, her hand running along the cool, chunky balustrade. Her bare feet moved silently on the worn treads. The air was even warmer on the second floor than it had been outside her apartment. Reaching the top of the stairs, she hesitated and some of her positive self-talk deserted her. Confronting a total stranger at two-thirty in the morning no longer seemed like such a great idea. Maybe she should just forget it; she could always do this during the day.

In the next instant, she chided herself for her cowardice. What was the worst that could happen?

Hannah strode over to the apartment door and, before she could change her mind, knocked firmly—three brief, sharp raps of her knuckles against the wood panels. She waited, aware that her heart was beating faster. She was being ridiculous. It was probably a sweet old lady who suffered from insomnia. She might even own one of those foot-driven antique spinning wheels. That could be the source of the thumping that woke her up each night. Even as she conjured up images of an apple-cheeked grandmother, the apartment door was yanked open and

Hannah found herself staring at a solid wall of hard, muscular, very ungrandmotherly maleness.

She took an involuntary step back.

Good Lord. He was close to six-and-a-half-feet tall and wore nothing but a pair of boxer shorts, the stretchy kind that hugged a guy's hips and outlined his masculine assets. Above the waist-band of his briefs, he had acres of bare, tanned skin. His arms were an incredible mix of bulging muscles and lean sinews. Her hands would probably be incapable of spanning those impressive biceps.

Her gaze drifted upward, past the hard ridges of his stomach to the flat planes of his chest, where a set of black military dog tags dangled from a slender chain and nestled in the shallow groove between his pectorals.

Hannah swallowed and forced herself to meet his eyes. They were dark and fathomless, and so completely bloodshot that she suspected he'd slept even less than she had during the past week. By the dim, overhead light, she could see the vivid scar that bisected one eyebrow and slashed upward into his dark hair.

She shivered, unable to shake the sense that she stood at the leading edge of a dark storm front. The very air around them seemed to tremble with turbulence. Hannah could almost feel a shift in the air pressure as she stared at him.

His face was lean and hard like the rest of him, all thrusting cheekbones and square jaw, covered in what must have been several days' growth of whiskers. Lines of weariness had etched themselves into the grooves alongside his mouth, and his eyes were red-rimmed with fatigue. His brows were drawn fiercely together as he swept her with a look that was both contemptuous and speculative.

"Who the hell are you?" His voice was low and deep, with a rasping quality to it, as if he'd just inhaled smoke. As he spoke, something resonated within Hannah, responding to the timbre of his voice and making her long to hear more.

He held a small glass filled with dark, amber liquid and as she watched, he deliberately raised the drink to his lips. She followed its path upward, fascinated when he drained the alcohol in one long swallow, his strong throat working smoothly. He palmed the glass in one hand and closed his eyes for a moment, as if to let the alcohol take effect. Hannah used the opportunity to get a good look at him. The only word that came to mind was *formidable*. He could have been straight out of Central Casting for the role of a dark avenger.

Everything about the guy was square, from his intelligent forehead and strong jaw, to the powerful thrust of his shoulders and the solid planes of his bare chest. Even his hands were square: big, capable hands with strong, blunt-tipped fingers. Her attention was drawn irresistibly downward, past his hips and over the length of his hard, sinewed thighs to where his left leg was encased in a black cast from mid-shin to his toes. It was a walking cast, and it took only an instant to figure out that the thumping noise she'd heard was the rounded block of hard plastic that protruded from the bottom of the cast. The guy had been pacing his floorboards.

"I'm Hannah Hartwell." The words came out in a breathless rush. She didn't extend her hand. She didn't want to touch him, didn't want to know what demons drove him to drink in the darkest hours of the night while pacing like a caged tiger. Instead, she crossed her arms in front of her, wishing she'd put on a bra *and* a sweatshirt. Wishing she'd never come at all. "I live downstairs."

His expression didn't change. He leaned one shoulder against the door frame and his eyes drifted slowly down the length of her body in a way that managed to be both insulting and appreciative at the same time. "There're only two reasons why a woman comes to a man's door in the middle of the night," he growled softly. "She's looking for sex, or money. Probably both." His lips twisted. "So, darlin'…how do you want it, and what's it gonna cost me?"

Hannah blinked but couldn't dispel the sudden images that swamped her imagination of this man, naked and glistening with sweat, providing pleasure to a woman. And not just any woman. Her.

In the next instant, she thrust the disturbing vision aside. It was just her sexual frustration and the remnants of her interrupted dream that had caused her imagination to surge. This man couldn't possibly know that she'd like nothing better than some really good sex. Or that he looked like he could get the job done, and then some. He was just trying to scare her. But no matter how big or how dangerous he appeared, she wouldn't let him intimidate her. She tipped her chin up and gave him what she hoped was a tolerant smile. "I'm not here for either of those things. I'm here to ask—"

"Just how old *are* you?"

"What?" Distracted, she could only stare at him.

"You look about sixteen." He straightened and took a step back, preparing to close the door in her face. "Get lost, kid. Whatever it is you're looking for, you sure as hell won't find it here."

"Wait." Without thinking, Hannah stepped forward and laid her hand on his forearm. Pain, white-hot and razor-sharp, sliced its way behind her eyes, causing her to gasp and snatch her hand away. Immediately, the pain vanished. Even so, the memory of it made her touch her fingers to her temple in an effort to reassure herself it was, indeed, gone.

Raising her eyes to his, she saw he'd gone white around the lips. Even as she watched, the empty tumbler slipped from his fingers and bounced on the wooden floor at his feet before rolling into the apartment. Neither of them made a move to retrieve it.

"Who the hell did you say you are?" His voice was no more than a low snarl.

Hannah tucked a strand of hair behind her ear and drew in a fortifying breath. "At a guess, I'd say I'm the answer to your prayers."

2

RANSOM BENNETT STARED at the girl, dumbfounded. What the hell had she done to him? In the split second she'd touched him, the dark, mushrooming pain in his head had disappeared. For one brief, glorious instant, he'd been completely pain free.

The incessant throbbing returned almost immediately, but—and maybe it was just his imagination—it seemed slightly less agonizing than it had been moments before. He could even focus on the girl without her image blurring.

Goddamn. Had he really thought she was just a kid? Now that his vision had cleared, he could see she was small, but there wasn't anything remotely childish about her. She looked like a damned Disney princess. Through the thin material of her skimpy top, he could see she didn't wear a bra. Her breasts were pert and perfectly formed, their nipples thrusting against the fabric. He'd always been attracted to big-busted women, but looking at her, he found himself wondering how those high, sweet mounds would fit into the palms of his hands. Just the fact that he could even think about sex was proof that he was feeling better.

She tilted her head back to look at him. Her eyes were big, and slightly tilted at the outer corners, thickly fringed with dark lashes. In the indistinct light of the hallway, he couldn't tell what color they were, but he was betting on blue. Baby blue, to match her small stature.

She was pixielike with her heart-shaped face and winged

eyebrows, but there was a calmness about her that told him she was older than he'd originally thought. His wisecrack about her wanting either sex or money hadn't seemed to faze her, either. Most women would be hightailing it back down the stairs. Unless she really *was* here for sex…but, no, he couldn't get that lucky.

Shit. The pain was increasing, blossoming behind his eyes to its former monstrous proportions. The girl's image wavered and then slowly separated into two identical, blurred shadows. He was going to throw up.

"Go home," he muttered, and staggered back into his apartment, using one hand to push blindly at the door. He inadvertently kicked the bourbon glass with his cast. He heard it skitter across the floor but didn't stop to pick it up. He'd be lucky if he made it to the bathroom.

The girl called something to him from the hallway, but he didn't respond, and he was only vaguely aware of her footsteps receding back down the staircase. The throbbing in his head had become a wrecking ball, turning whatever gray matter he had left to mush and threatening to disintegrate his skull. He barely made it into the bathroom before his stomach rid itself of the six aspirin, two prescription painkillers and three shots of bourbon he'd guzzled earlier.

Groaning, he rinsed his mouth and splashed cool water over his face, letting it trickle down his neck and over his chest. The droplets were like ice water against his sensitized skin. He groped his way back to his bedroom and collapsed across the bed, keeping his eyes closed. If he opened them, the room would start spinning and he'd be back in the bathroom, but this time he'd have nothing left to offer.

The excruciating pain in his head was even worse lying down, but Ransom didn't think he had the strength to stand up, much less walk it off. To top it off, it was hot as hell in the bedroom. There was an air-conditioning unit in one of the windows, but to his overly sensitive hearing it had seemed abnormally loud, like a jet engine, so he'd turned it off.

Cracking an eyelid, he peered through the gloom of the bedroom to his nightstand, where he'd left the bottle of Jim Beam next to a small container of prescription painkillers. What was it the girl had said? *I'm the answer to your prayers.* Yeah, right. The only thing he prayed for was enough whiskey to make him pass out.

Propping himself on one elbow, he reached for the bottle, only to have it lifted and placed out of his reach. With a soft growl, he shifted his gaze to the girl who stood beside the bed looking down at him. Hadn't he shut the door? Locked it? Damn, he couldn't think straight. He could barely muster enough energy to be indignant at her unwelcome intrusion.

"Darlin'," he said, his voice raspy with pain, "you're either extremely brave or incredibly stupid."

She cocked her head and smiled uncertainly. "I beg your pardon?"

"It's obvious you don't have the slightest instinct for self-preservation."

That made her smile. "I hardly think you're in any position to harm me, and trust me when I say liquor is not the answer. Jeez, it's so hot in here. No wonder you feel sick. How can you stand it?"

Before he could protest, she stepped over to the air conditioner and flipped it on. He groaned as it whirred to life. He might as well be lying on the flight deck of an aircraft carrier. But the cool blast of air that wafted over his body felt good.

"Here," the girl murmured. "I've brought you something that will help the pain."

He felt the mattress sag as she sat down on the edge of the bed and placed something cool and soothing over his brow. It had an odd smell to it, but when he would have dragged it off, she laid her hand over his to stop him.

"Leave it on," she chastised softly. "It's just an herbal compress."

"Where'd it come from?" he growled ungraciously.

"I have several in my apartment," she explained, but didn't move her hand from where it covered his.

The pain didn't completely vanish as it had before when she'd touched him, but it loosened its grip on him enough that the nausea subsided. He could even open both eyes. Pale shafts of moonlight spilled in through the windows behind the bed, illuminating the room in shades of silver and gray.

The girl sat beside him, her expression one of concern and compassion. Blond hair framed her face and fell in loose waves around her shoulders. Her fingers were cool, yet he had the oddest sensation of heat where she touched him. It was like one of those peppermint-scented muscle-rub ointments, hot and cold all at the same time.

"Who are you?" His voice sounded like rough sandpaper compared to hers. "And don't give me any bullshit."

She arched a brow at him. In the darkness, her pupils were enormous, drowning out the paler irises that surrounded them. "I already told you, I'm Hannah Hartwell. I just moved in downstairs. And you are…?"

"Ransom. Bennett."

She removed her hand from where it rested on top of his and used her fingers to smooth the compress over his forehead instead. Ransom only barely restrained himself from snatching it back and pressing it against his flesh. There was something about her touch… The wrecking ball was definitely receding, leaving a dull, throbbing ache in its stead. He could handle that. Dull and throbbing was a huge improvement over total incapacitation.

"Ransom, huh?" She swept him an approving glance and gave him a teasing smile. "As in…handsome Ransom?"

He snorted. He was pretty sure no one could call him handsome, especially in his present state. He felt like an animal. He probably smelled like one, too. He didn't even bother to respond to her comment, just gave her his best I'm-not-amused glower.

Her smile faded and she cleared her throat. "I came up here to tell you that you've woken me up every night this week with your pacing. But I'd no idea…"

Her voice trailed off, and Ransom could guess what her thoughts were. "What?" he asked roughly, studying her face. "That you had a boozer for a neighbor?"

She gave him a quizzical look but didn't stop the movement of her fingers over his forehead. "Is that what you do for the pain? Drink yourself into oblivion?"

He snorted. "Only if I'm lucky."

"Hmm."

She didn't say anything else, just continued to stroke her fingertips over the compress. He wanted to protest, tell her to get lost and leave him alone with his misery, but the words stuck in his throat. Besides, she smelled good and it wasn't too much of a hardship to have her leaning over him, rubbing his brow. When her fingers slid to his temples, he stiffened.

"Shh," she soothed. "Relax. Close your eyes."

Her fingertips traced circular patterns over his temples, and Ransom heard himself groan with pleasure. "Jesus," he whispered raggedly, "what are you, some kind of witch?"

She laughed softly, a warm, throaty sound that made him open his eyes and reassess her. In the darkness, her face was a pale, oval blur. Her neck was slender, and he had the strongest urge to run his fingers along the fragile line of her collarbone. When she leaned forward to push her fingers deeper into his hair, her top gaped away and he glimpsed the shadowed valley between her breasts.

"I'm a sensitive," she murmured. Her fingers massaged the area behind his ears and he almost purred in satisfaction.

"Oh, yeah?" His voice sounded drowsy, even to his own ears.

If she kept this up, he just might fall asleep. Except that, Christ, he could *smell* her. The scent was light and feminine and had nothing to do with artificial perfumes or flowery bath products. It was *her,* and the fragrance completely distracted him, made him think of raw, uninhibited sex. With her.

She was still leaning over him, massaging his temples, and he could picture it so damned clearly, he almost groaned aloud with desire. Her, naked and straddling his hips while he cupped her sweet ass cheeks in his hands, riding him hard as he drove her to a screaming climax.

Whoa.

He slammed the door shut on the image, as arousing and tantalizing as it was, and struggled to recall what they'd been talking about. Oh, yeah. She'd said she was a sensitive. He couldn't prevent a wry chuckle. "Women tell me I'm *in*sensitive."

Which was pretty ironic, really, considering how ultrasensitive he'd been to any external stimuli, at least since he'd been released from the hospital. One minute, he'd be okay and the next he'd be down for the count. Light, noise, even motion was enough to cause him agonizing pain. The doctors said the migraines were a direct result of the head injury he'd sustained, and that they'd eventually go away, but until now, he hadn't detected much improvement. He was lucky if he went a full day without one.

"Imagine that," Hannah murmured in response to his comment, but Ransom thought he detected humor in her voice. "I meant that sometimes I can feel other people's pain."

"No shit." Now he'd heard everything. It wasn't true, of course, because if she'd felt even a modicum of the pain he'd endured for the past month, she'd have already done herself in. "That must really suck."

"Hmm. Sometimes." She peeled the compress away from his skin and ran her finger lightly over the scar that tracked its way across his forehead. "This wound…it's healed on the outside, but there's still damage underneath."

Ransom could swear the newly healed scar throbbed when she touched it. "What, you have X-ray vision, too?"

She smiled at that, a cheeky grin that made her eyes dance with humor. "Mmm-hmm. I know exactly what's beneath your boxers, for example."

"*Jesus.*" The word erupted on a strangled laugh. "You don't know me nearly well enough for that."

Something he'd definitely need to take care of.

Ransom had no idea where that thought had come from, but as Hannah slid her gaze over him, letting it linger on his crotch for about two seconds longer than was polite, he realized he was completely turned on. Which made him realize something even more amazing: his headache was nearly gone. Aside from a dull ache right between his eyes, he felt almost normal.

Hannah folded the compress neatly in her hand and then, as Ransom watched, she dropped her head between her knees and inhaled deeply several times, long and slow. He eased himself up onto one elbow and peered over at her. What the hell?

"Hey, you okay?"

She waved a dismissive hand in his direction, and then sat upright with one more deep, indrawn breath. She blew it out, slow and controlled, and then turned to look at him. "It's nothing, just a little dizziness," she assured him. "It happens sometimes when I do a hands-on treatment."

Ransom watched through narrowed eyes as she composed herself and then stood up. In another minute she'd be gone.

"How'd you do that?"

She looked at him, all innocence, but he saw her gaze slide back over the length of his body and linger briefly on the spot where his traitorous body was responding to her nearness. "Do what?"

"Get rid of the migraine." Forcing himself to ignore his

physical reaction to her, he turned his head experimentally from side to side, but his vision didn't blur and his stomach stayed put. No blinding pain shot through his scalp.

"Probably just coincidence," she said, and made to turn away.

Ransom reached out and caught her wrist. Instinct told him she was lying. She was hiding something and he was going to find out what it was. Her skin was warm and satiny beneath his fingers, her bones so fragile that he could crush them easily. He loosened his hold but didn't release her. "So you're saying you had nothing to do with my headache disappearing?"

She hesitated, a barely discernible pause, but Ransom didn't miss it.

"Maybe I did." She tried to tug her arm free. "But then again maybe all you needed was a cool compress."

Ransom snorted and released her wrist. She was totally bull-shitting him, but apart from calling her a liar, there wasn't anything he could do about it. And if he thought about it rationally, he didn't actually *believe* she'd healed him with her touch. That sort of thing only happened on television, and usually involved alien beings.

But there was no denying he felt better. It was probably just the bourbon finally kicking in, or the pain meds he'd taken around midnight. But he didn't really believe that, either.

"Of course. A cool compress. Why didn't I think of that?"

"Well, the important thing is that you feel better," she said brightly, ignoring his sarcasm. "Maybe now we can both get some sleep."

Yeah, right. As if the constant migraines weren't punishment enough, the nightmares were even worse. As much as his body craved sleep, he dreaded closing his eyes. Because when he did, he saw the faces of his men and relived the swift, bloody ambush that had decimated their four-man Delta Force team. They'd been traveling through a rugged, mountainous region in northern Afghanistan when they'd been attacked by a veritable army of

Taliban terrorists. His communications specialist had been killed, and the remaining two team members captured, despite fierce resistance. A mortar round had blown him thirty feet from the firefight and knocked him unconscious. Either the attackers hadn't seen him, or they'd figured he was dead.

He had no recollection of being extracted from the region, or even being medevaced to the United States, but he remembered every detail of that deadly firefight in slow-moving, excruciating detail. Even the prescription sleeping tablets didn't stand a chance against the Technicolor replays that invaded his dreams. They dragged him, raw and aching and coated with sweat, into wakefulness. Every night.

The dreams weren't fueled by fear, but by his own failure to adequately assess the situation that had ultimately led to the defeat and capture of his team. He should have anticipated the attack, should have prevented it. He simply couldn't stop thinking about it, or analyzing what he might have done differently. He'd spent the better part of his life training to be a Delta Force operator, and not just a good one, but the best one. And yet, in the end, he'd let his men down.

He'd taken to pacing the floors, but that only made the migraines worse. If he was lucky, the bourbon knocked back both the headaches and the nightmares, but mostly it just made him sick. Like tonight.

The doctors had told him the head injury would heal, but it had been six goddamned weeks and he felt worse than ever.

Until now.

Until this girl—woman, he amended silently—had shown up on his doorstep, like some kind of freaking angel. He didn't know how she did it, but she'd gotten rid of the unrelenting pain. Still, as much as his body craved sleep, there was no way he'd willingly return to the dark realm that rivaled any version of hell that Clive Barker could create.

"I am tired," he acknowledged roughly, breaking the silence. He lowered himself back on the mattress and allowed his gaze to drift over her. "But the last thing I want to do is sleep."

3

HANNAH GAPED at him. Lying across the bed with his arms bent behind his head displayed his impressive biceps to full advantage. He was supremely male, from the light furring beneath his arms, to the toned muscles that fingered their way along his rib cage, to the suggestion in his dark eyes that transformed his face from unapproachable to irresistible.

Her eyes lingered on his mouth, softer and more inviting without the deep furrows of pain on either side of it, and her hand itched to trace along the fullness of his bottom lip. Not to mention the masculine promise she'd seen stirring beneath the knit fabric of his boxers. The sight didn't alarm her. Rather, it brought the erotic dream rushing back in full force.

With a sense of shock and growing horror, Hannah realized she was becoming aroused just looking at him. He smelled good, too. Nothing artificial, just stark earthy male. She wondered what his skin would taste like beneath her lips. A languorous heat was building at her core, and her breasts felt tight and achy. She could almost feel that smooth, heated flesh under her hands.

She was worse than pathetic. The guy was obviously ill, and here she was wondering what it would be like to cover his body with her own. Most women would probably be repelled by his coarseness; count on her to find it attractive.

Dragging her focus away, she reached blindly for the bottle

of bourbon on his bedside table and took a hefty swig, welcoming the burning sensation of the alcohol as it seared its way down her throat.

"Hey, easy," he murmured, as she spluttered and her eyes began to water. He took the bottle from her unresisting fingers and placed it back on the table. "Just how old are you, anyway?"

Hannah gasped for breath and sat back down on the edge of the mattress, swiping a finger across her lips. The bourbon left a warm, tingling sensation in her stomach, and the taste of it in her mouth wasn't entirely unpleasant. Eyeing the bottle, she tucked a loose tendril of hair behind one ear.

"I'm twenty-five," she said, when she could finally catch her breath. "I may be small, but I'm legal."

Ransom's eyes gleamed in the indistinct light. "Lady," he growled, "you're not small. You're damned near microscopic."

Okay, she'd heard the same sentiment hundreds of times before and she'd accepted the fact she was never going to have a body like Jennifer Lopez, but hearing it from this guy was somehow demoralizing. As if she really was less than a woman. His words had the effect of bringing her back to her senses. The heat unfurling in her center didn't quite cool, but it no longer threatened to melt her better judgment.

"Right. I—I should probably go," she murmured, and stood up. "You really should get some rest."

She turned away, lest he see how dangerously close she had come to touching him in a way that had nothing to do with comfort or healing. But she'd only taken one step when he reached out and caught her arm, his hand sliding from elbow to wrist in a heated glide.

"Wait."

She did, but didn't turn around.

"What if my headache returns?"

"Then you should see a doctor."

He made a small sound of annoyance. "I've seen a doctor. Several, in fact. I'd rather see you."

She did turn around then, knowing her expression was wary. "What do you mean?"

His hand encircled her wrist and his thumb rubbed absently against the sensitive skin on the underside. He probably wasn't even aware he was doing it. One arm was still bent behind his head. His dog tags had slid sideways, off his chest, to rest just beneath his armpit, dark and dull against his skin. Hannah wondered briefly why they were black, and not the standard, steel-colored tags.

"Your, uh, compress did the trick, apparently." He gave a soft huff of disbelieving laughter. "I just thought... Hell, I don't know what I thought. That maybe you could give me a supply of them. Or something."

Hannah shifted her attention to his face. His expression was carefully shuttered, as if he didn't want her to see how desperately he wanted help. But it was there in the stillness of his body, even as his thumb smoothed over her wrist.

"Okay." The single word came out in a rush. "Come downstairs tomorrow morning. Ten o'clock. Wear something comfortable." She couldn't prevent one long sweep of his body with her eyes. "Just make sure you're decent."

He released her wrist, and it was all Hannah could do not to massage the spot where his fingers had been. He raised himself up on one elbow, his expression dubious.

"Why? What do you have in mind?"

Hannah arched a brow at him. "Do you want my help, or not?"

"Yes...no. It depends."

She shrugged. "Fine. Don't come, then. I was going to offer you treatments, but since you can't seem to make up your mind, you can just come into the shop once it's opened and pay full price, like all my other customers."

"Treatments? Just what the hell is it you do?" He was looking at her as if he suspected her of turning tricks in the first-floor shop.

Hannah's first instinct was to turn on her heel and leave. Even before the arrest her practice had been viewed with suspicion, and it irritated the hell out of her. Instead, she bit her tongue on the sharp retort that hovered there, and gave him a tolerant look. "Energy healing. I'm a Reiki practitioner."

He fell back with a disgusted snort. "Yeah. Okay. Let me just run right downstairs and get my free energy healing now, before you're completely overrun with customers."

Hannah didn't even flinch at the harsh cynicism in his voice. If the unpleasantness she'd left behind in South Boston had taught her one thing, it was to school her emotions. Sully had tried to destroy her business and herself along with it. At the lowest point in the long ordeal to clear her name, the only thing she'd had left was her dignity. If Sully, with his criminal-tough demeanor, couldn't make her lose her composure, neither would this man.

"Like I said," she replied easily, "it makes no difference to me. I have a lot of work to do between now and the end of next week. Providing you with daily treatments would just get in the way of that. So…good luck with everything."

"Wait."

This time, Hannah turned around and faced him. "Why? So you can mock me some more?" She made a sound of dismissal. "You don't have to believe in energy healing, Mr. Bennett, but before you say another insulting word, take a good, hard look at yourself." She swept a hand toward him. "You're miserable. I mean, jeez, when's the last time you ate something healthy? Or got a full night's rest? Or even felt human? What exactly do you have to lose by giving it a try?"

He was silent.

Hannah blew out her breath. As much as her head told her to walk away, her chest tightened in sympathy for this man who, despite his tough appearance and gruff manner, obviously needed help. Help that she could give him. Not that she was all that keen on having him around. He was too big. Too male.

Too completely tempting.

But she believed in karma. If she deliberately turned her back on this man, it could come back to haunt her one day. And she needed all the good karma she could get.

"Tomorrow morning, ten o'clock," she repeated briskly. "I'll help you, but you have to do something for me, in return."

He peered suspiciously at her. "Like what?"

"I need to get the shop ready for opening day. There's painting that needs to be done, and I need shelving units and ceiling fans installed, and a dozen other things." She glanced at his cast and smiled wryly. "Your leg doesn't seem to slow you down too much, if your nocturnal pacing is anything to go by. If you can help me fix up the shop, then I guarantee I'll have you feeling like a new man in, oh, three weeks."

Even in the dim light, she could see his amused smile. "A new man in three weeks, huh? Kinda hard to turn down an offer like that. Okay, fine. I'll be there." He yawned hugely, and his eyes drifted closed.

"Great." She turned to leave but couldn't resist one last peek at him from the doorway of the bedroom. He lay sprawled across the mattress like a darkly decadent offering. Moonlight slanted in through the window behind him, gilding his body in silver.

She hesitated.

"Tomorrow." His voice was husky with the sleep, and it seemed to Hannah that the word hung on the air, like a promise.

She fled.

It wasn't until she was back in her own bed that she wondered what on earth she had just done. She stared at the ceiling and pictured Ransom, muscular and nearly naked, spread out on his bed directly over her. She recalled the hard ridge of flesh she'd seen stirring beneath his snug boxers, and just like that, desire swamped her, sharp and fierce.

Closing her eyes, she saw again the hard ripples of his abdomen and the smooth, flat planes of his muscled chest. She saw his eyes, dark and fathomless, heard his whiskey-rough voice as he taunted her.

What would it be like to be with a man like Ransom Bennett? There would be nothing insipid or tentative about his lovemaking. He'd be strong and sure, forceful even. She imagined herself clinging to him, legs wrapped around his hips as he surged into her and, almost without realizing it, she slid a hand beneath the elastic waistband of the men's boxers she wore.

She was drenched with moisture. Swollen. Pulsing with need. With one hand at her breast, she pinched her nipple through the thin material of her top until it stood out, stiff and aching. Her other hand moved over her damp curls until she found the apex of her desire. She swirled her fingers over the hard, aching nub, and a whimper of pleasure escaped her lips.

But it wasn't enough.

Her thighs fell apart and she cupped herself, imagining it was Ransom's hand that touched her so intimately, Ransom's fingers pushing inside her, stretching her, filling her. She arched her back and, in her mind's eye, he came over her, thrusting into her and causing her to cry out with unbearable pleasure. At the same time, she used her thumb to tease the small, slick rise of flesh that tormented her. She was racing toward release, her entire body taut with anticipation, drawn on a fine bow of incredible sensation.

When her orgasm hit her, she cried out, her hips thrusting helplessly against her hand, until finally, the last tremors subsided, leaving her trembling and weak.

Her breathing still uneven, she curled on her side and bunched the pillow beneath her cheek. In her dream, her lover had been faceless. But just now, as she'd pleasured herself, her imaginary partner had had a face, and it was darkly handsome.

Ransom Bennett.

A man she didn't even know. And she'd just agreed to provide him with free treatments, every day for the next three weeks.

She was so screwed.

4

RANSOM PEERED at his reflection in the mirror over the small bathroom sink. He looked like hell. He'd showered and shaved the beard growth from his jaw, but even five hours of uninterrupted sleep hadn't been enough to erase the redness from his eyes, or the shadows beneath them. His head hurt, a dull, persistent throbbing behind his eyes that he knew would increase as the day wore on.

On the nights when he did manage to get some sleep, he generally woke up with a clear head and minimal pain, at least for a few good hours. Those were the mornings he'd leave the house before dawn and head to Camp Lejeune. The Marine Corps base wasn't his primary base of operations. Hell, he wasn't even in the Marine Corps, but the camp maintained a state-of-the-art facility for the training and deployment of special operations forces, including Delta Force.

The war room, located inside their compound, was where Ransom spent endless hours poring over detailed topography maps and satellite images of Afghanistan. Two Delta Force crypt-analysts—part of the so-called Funny Platoon—were working 24/7 to evaluate and decipher communications intercepted by that supersecret intelligence unit. The detailed analysis, combined with the time Ransom spent at the shooting range, only aggravated his headaches, but there was no other option. Only death—or something damn close to it—would keep him from either the war room or the range.

Right now, the missing men were the only thing that mattered. His commanding officer, Colonel Lindahl, had already given him a warning order, a verbal notification that he'd be getting a mission. A new team had been carefully put together—six men, including himself, whose unique capabilities would guarantee success.

Four weeks had passed since the ambush. Four weeks since his men had been taken hostage and Ransom had woken up in a military hospital. He'd suffered a mild stress fracture in his foot, and the doctors had put him in a cast as a precaution, but it was the head wound that was causing him the most pain. His doctor had assured him the injury had almost entirely healed, but the migraines persisted. Ransom refused to tell anyone just how bad the headaches had become, knowing his commanding officer would sideline him for any combat mission if he wasn't completely recovered.

Nothing was more important to Ransom than returning to Afghanistan to extract his men. He was better qualified to locate them than any other operator. He'd been part of the first team of Delta operators to infiltrate the country following the September 11 attacks, and had spent the better part of the past seven years over there, building relationships with the local tribal leaders and gathering intel. If anyone knew the rugged northern regions, he did.

Since receiving the warning order, he and the rest of his unit had begun planning the rescue operation, code name *Formidable Force*. It would involve two other Delta teams, as well as support from other Special Forces units already in the box, the area of operations.

The teams had trained and prepared for every contingency. While they still didn't know the exact location of the hostages, they'd narrowed it down to three possibilities. The U.S. Army owned hundreds of square miles of sprawling wilderness in North Carolina. Deep behind the razor-wire fencing that surrounded the rough country, they'd built replicas of the three strongholds and had reenacted how the rescue would unfold. They'd run through everything, from the nighttime parachute drop into enemy territory, to the extraction, knowing they would be carrying two severely injured operators. They were as ready as they would ever be.

The plan was twofold: extract his captured men and deal with the tribal warlord who had betrayed them. All they needed was a thumbs-up from senior leadership, and they'd be boots on the ground within twenty-four hours. This time, failure would not be an option.

Reaching up, he traced his fingertips over the scar above his eye. It wasn't painful to the touch; the ache went much deeper than the surface. He recalled again the girl's fingers as she'd stroked the injury, and how he hadn't wanted her to stop. Last night, he'd have sworn she had some kind of special powers, her touch cathartic. But last night he'd been more than a little shit-faced.

Now, with morning sunlight slanting in through the edges of the drawn shades, and his stomach slightly queasy from too much bourbon and not enough food, he knew it was nothing more than a bunch of crap. It had been a combination of the painkillers and alcohol that had finally dulled his pain and allowed him to sleep, not the girl.

Definitely not the girl.

Ransom fastened his watch around his wrist as he checked the time. Almost ten o'clock. He scrubbed his hands over his face. The night's events were a little hazy, but he remembered enough to realize he should probably feel embarrassed.

Instead, a memory of smooth, scented skin and soft breasts flashed through his mind, and his body stirred in response, but he determinedly tamped it down. He didn't need that kind of entanglement. Not now.

What had she said? That she'd have him feeling like a new man in just three weeks? He snorted. What the hell, he'd give it a shot.

If she could reduce the intensity of the headaches by even a small margin, it would be well worth it. He'd even help her fix up the little storefront. A couple hours each day wouldn't jeopardize the mission, and his body would welcome the physical activity.

He could still see Abdul Alkazar's face as he'd pledged his support in helping U.S. troops rid the area of a Taliban choke hold. The tribal warlord had welcomed Ransom into his home and broken bread with him. He'd guaranteed Ransom and his men safe passage through his territories. Hell, he'd been paid good money in return for his loyalty. Instead, he'd betrayed them, and now one operator was dead and the fate of two more was unknown.

If his two men were still alive, Ransom and his team would find them and bring them home. The only thing jeopardizing his role in the mission was the headaches. He needed to recover, and he needed to do it quickly.

HANNAH GLANCED at the little clock over the stove. Fifteen minutes past ten. Would he show? Last night, she'd have staked her last dollar on the fact that he'd been sincere when he'd agreed to let her help him. But now, with dust motes swirling lazily in a shaft of morning sunlight, the previous evening might have been no more than a figment of her overactive imagination. However, just in case it hadn't been, she'd taken extra care with her appearance that morning.

She wore her favorite tiered gypsy skirt, with small coins stitched into the turquoise fabric. It swirled around her ankles with each movement, making her feel like an exotic, Eastern dancer. Paired with a figure-hugging, lace-edged camisole, the result was both feminine and flirtatious. Chandelier earrings hung from her earlobes, and a slender chain with a pale blue, celestite crystal nestled in the valley between her breasts. The only thing missing was the gorgeous amethyst ring that Hannah had inherited upon her grandmother's death.

Her aunt Elle had told her that the stone was extremely powerful and contained protective properties, as well as healing and cleansing powers. The stone had become loose in the setting, so Hannah wouldn't wear it until she had a chance to have it repaired. But she missed its familiar weight and wished she'd put it on anyway. Some might say it was a wasted effort, since she'd have to remove the jewelry when it came time to perform Ransom's treatment, but Hannah had wanted to look nice.

For him.

Which was ludicrous. He was probably one of those die-hard marines who had a woman in every port, and was incapable of making a commitment except to his regiment. Besides, the last thing she needed was a man in her life. But sometimes, what you needed and what you *wanted* were two entirely different things. And last night, she'd wanted Ransom Bennett in a bad way.

The slender bangles around her wrist tinkled softly as she turned the heat off under the whistling teakettle. As she reached into an overhead cupboard for a teacup, a movement outside the kitchen window caught her attention. With the cup in one hand, she craned her neck and peered through the curtains at the house next door. In the next instant, the fragile teacup dropped from her nerveless fingers and shattered on the tiled floor.

Hannah flattened herself against the wall beside the window, out of sight of the man who stood in the second-floor window of the neighboring house, watching her through a pair of binoculars. Her heart thudded hard in her chest.

Maybe she'd imagined it. Maybe it was just her overactive imagination, playing tricks on her.

Recalling the image, she shivered. No, it had definitely been a man standing just inside the window, and there was no doubt in her mind that he'd been watching her through a big old pair of field glasses. The question was, *why?*

Had Sully found her?

In the next instant, she chastised herself. If Sully *had* located her, he wouldn't waste his time spying on her from a neighboring house. He'd come through her front door like a military tank, blasting aside her resistance and squashing her like a bug. The thought actually gave her a little courage.

Cautiously, Hannah parted the edge of the curtain and peeked at the house, but the window was now empty. There wasn't any sign of activity. She drew in a calming breath. The man hadn't been Sully, she was certain of that. He'd had a completely different build than Sully's rugged frame. Still, the knowledge that the man in the house next door was a Peeping Tom wasn't exactly comforting, either. She made a mental note to purchase blinds for the windows as soon as possible, even as she tried to recall how many times she'd paraded bare assed through the little apartment.

Letting the curtain fall back into place, she eyed the broken china on the floor with regret. With a sigh, she bent down to scoop the fragments together, then cocked her head and listened.

Thump. Thump. Thump.

Unless she was mistaken, Ransom Bennett was on his way downstairs. Working quickly, Hannah picked up the broken shards and then, mindful of her bare feet, gingerly stepped over the spot to discard them in the trash. Surveying the tiny kitchen and adjoining living area, she grimaced. She'd unpacked her boxes for these two rooms but hadn't quite found permanent homes for her assortment of artwork and her collection of Tibetan singing bowls. They covered the countertops and were stacked haphazardly along the walls. Nothing could disguise that her apartment was a total disaster. Even her furniture was covered with the contents of the boxes. The only clear space was the path she'd made through to the empty guest bedroom, where she'd set up a massage table. Not that she was actually going to touch him. She shivered. No way.

She heard him make his way down the stairwell a brief minute before he knocked at her door. Hannah drew in a deep breath and tried to ignore the fluttering sensation low in her belly, a combination of trepidation and anticipation that caused her heart rate to kick up a notch. She tucked her hair behind her ears and smoothed a hand down over her peasant-style skirt, and then opened the door.

He sized her up with one dark glance, before stepping past her. Hannah swallowed hard, then closed the door and leaned against it. Ransom stood just inside the room, his gaze sweeping over the jumble of boxes and the partially unpacked belongings that covered nearly every surface. He wore a faded green army T-shirt and cargo shorts, and a flip-flop sandal on his bare foot. Even fully dressed, with morning sunlight slanting through the kitchen windows, he exuded a raw, dark power. With his height and broad shoulders, the already cluttered room bordered on claustrophobic.

"You sure you're moving in?" he asked, arching an eyebrow at her. "Looks to me like you haven't made up your mind."

Hannah brushed past him to lift the teakettle and pour steaming water into a small teapot she'd placed on the counter. "I haven't had much time to unpack," she explained, trying to ignore the way her heart pounded. "My first priority is getting the shop ready." She reached up to pull another teacup down from the cupboard. "I really appreciate any help you can give me. Oh!"

With a small yelp of pain, she lifted her bare foot and stared at the tiny sliver of porcelain embedded in her arch. Acutely aware of the man who stood watching her, she hobbled over to one of the bar stools near the counter and climbed onto it.

"I broke a teacup," she explained, "but didn't have time to clean up properly."

Before she could guess his intent, Ransom captured her injured foot in one big hand and bent over to inspect it more closely. His other hand cupped her calf muscle beneath the hem of her skirt.

Hannah watched in fascination as he turned her foot toward the light, mildly embarrassed by the intimate contact, but also a little pleased that she'd applied a coat of cherry-red nail polish to her toes. When he brushed his thumb across the silver band that encircled her middle toe, it was all she could do not to squirm on the bar stool. His hand was warm, and so big that it easily encompassed her foot. She tried unsuccessfully to pull it free.

"It's nothing," she protested weakly. "Really, I'm fine. It's just a little bit of glass."

He glanced up at her face. "You wouldn't want it to get infected."

With a gentleness she wouldn't have believed possible, he plucked the offending sliver from her foot, and then carefully squeezed the area until a small droplet of blood appeared.

"You're not from around here," he said, his eyes on the bottom of her foot.

The statement was made casually, and as much as Hannah told herself it was a perfectly normal observation—as innocuous as commenting on the weather—it unnerved her. She'd rehearsed a little speech just for this occasion. Something about how she'd recently returned from a spiritual trip to India.

"No," she agreed. "I'm from up north." Inwardly, she groaned. Where had that come from? It was definitely not the response she'd practiced.

Ransom chuckled. "Yeah, I got that from your accent. I mean where, specifically?" His eyes slid briefly back to her face, studying her response. "Sounds like a Massachusetts dialect."

Damn, damn, damn.

"Why do you say that? I mean, I could be from anywhere in New England. Maybe it's a Vermont accent," she protested weakly. "Or maybe I'm from Rhode Island."

"Not likely," he snorted. "I have a couple of good friends from up there. I know a Boston accent when I hear it."

"It's been a long time since I've lived there," she lied. "I'm surprised I even have an accent, that's how long it's been since I left Massachusetts."

"Uh-huh." Leaning over the counter, he tore a paper towel from the dispenser and swabbed the area. Satisfied, he released her foot and straightened. "Do you have any Band-Aids?"

"Uh, no, I don't think so."

A smile lifted one side of his mouth. "Of course not. You'll just heal it with your psychic energy, right?"

Hannah slid off the stool and smoothed her skirt, and told herself she wasn't the least bit affected by the way the wry smile changed his face. "Go ahead, make fun. We'll see who has the last laugh." She indicated the teapot. "Would you mind pouring the tea for me? It should be steeped enough by now."

While he poured the tea, she slid her feet into a pair of worn sneakers. She didn't miss Ransom's sidelong scrutiny of her toes, which poked out through frayed holes along the sides. She wondered if he was as aware of her as she was of him. She hoped not.

Thankfully he'd dropped the subject of where she'd lived before she came to Cliftondale. Not that she had anything to hide, because she didn't. After all, the charges against her had been thrown out for lack of evidence. But despite the fact that she'd been absolved of any wrongdoing, she couldn't help but feel a certain amount of shame over what had happened.

Telling herself that she'd been a victim of corrupt power didn't make her feel any better, either. The Boston newspapers had run daily stories about her arrest and subsequent trial, and she had no doubt that if the courts had found her guilty of soliciting sex in her shop, the press would have declared her a charlatan, as well as a prostitute. No, she had no desire to reveal to Ransom where she'd lived before she came to Cliftondale.

Or why she'd left.

5

HANNAH STUDIED Ransom covertly while she worked the lacings on her sneakers. He looked completely out of place in her little kitchen. With his height and his broad shoulders, he dominated the small space. She watched as he set the kettle back on the stove and then carried the teapot and cup over to the bar stools.

He set them down and turned his attention to the living room. "If you'd like, I could help you straighten up in here."

Just the thought of this man performing such a cozy, domestic task caused her stomach to flutter. It was like asking a timber wolf to act like a lapdog.

"No, thanks," she said, softening her rejection with a smile. "It usually takes me a while to figure out where things belong. I need to live in a space for a couple of weeks to learn where the happy spots are."

"The happy spots?" Ransom's voice sounded strangled, and Hannah looked questioningly at him. She didn't know him well but suspected he was trying not to burst out laughing.

"Yes. You know, where the natural flow of energy is, and where I should place things to achieve the best harmony. The happy spots."

"Ah. Like feng shui."

"Exactly." Hannah shot him a look of surprised approval, then reached past him and handed him the cup of tea. "Here, I want you to drink this."

"What is it?" He looked suspiciously at the steaming cup she held out to him.

"It's a Chinese herbal tea. Don't worry, there's nothing harmful in it, but it helps migraines." She held it gingerly by the saucer. "Go ahead…"

Ransom took the cup. It looked ridiculously fragile in his big hands. He sniffed it, and looked at Hannah over the rim. Her breath caught. His eyes weren't dark, as she'd first thought. They were a shade of blue so dark that they bordered on black and reminded her of the turbulent waters of the Atlantic on a stormy day. She watched, enthralled, as he took a tentative sip, his lips flexing in a way that made her wonder what it would be like to kiss him. He took a second sip and considered it.

"Not bad, but it's a little bitter."

Hannah dragged her attention away from his mouth. "You'll get used to it. I'll give you some to take upstairs with you. You should drink it at least three times a day, but none after two o'clock or the caffeine will keep you awake."

He made a sound that sounded suspiciously like a snort. "Yeah," he muttered, "if only it was caffeine that kept me awake."

"How *is* your headache this morning?"

He shrugged and took a long swallow of the tea, grimacing. "About the same. By dinnertime, I'll be wishing I had a loaded gun."

Remembering the dog tags she'd seen dangling around his neck, Hannah glanced at him in alarm. "You don't, do you? Have a firearm, I mean?"

Instead of answering, he took another long swallow and set the empty teacup down on top of the nearest box. "Look," he ground out, "do you think we could just get on with this?"

Hannah looked sharply at him. She noted the shadows beneath his eyes and how he squinted against the sunlight that filtered through the kitchen window and fell across the floor in bright squares.

"Sorry," she mumbled. "There were no shades on these windows when I moved in, and I haven't had a chance to install any yet. It's better in the spare room." She moved through the living room, indicating he should come with her. "Why don't you come in here and lie down?"

Ransom followed her. He stepped into the spare room and his sweeping gaze missed nothing. Wood-slatted shades had been drawn closed over the windows. In stark contrast to the rest of her apartment, this room was dark and virtually empty except for a massage table and chair in the center. Soft music played from a small CD player on the windowsill, and a blanket lay folded neatly on a second chair near the door.

"I'm not sure why, but I kept this room clear of clutter," Hannah mused. "It must have been fate, huh?"

Ransom's lips twisted, but he didn't answer. Instead, he stepped over to the table. "Do you want me on my back, or on my stomach?"

His words caused Hannah's imagination to surge, and she determinedly pushed down the erotic images that sprang to mind. "Um, on your back, please," she said, striving for a professional tone.

Performing Reiki treatments would be so much easier once she had her shop open and was surrounded by the tools and products of her profession. Here, in the spare bedroom of her apartment, the atmosphere seemed overly intimate. She waited while he settled himself on the table. He was so big that his feet hung over the edge.

"Here," she said, carefully lifting his injured leg, "let me adjust this extender." She slid a small extension panel out from the end of the cushioned table to support his feet. "Is that better? Are you in pain?"

He raised his head and considered her briefly. Hannah wasn't certain, but she thought she detected a hint of dimple in one lean cheek. "You tell me—you're the sensitive."

Hannah gave him a tolerant look, but couldn't resist a smile as she laid one hand on his cast. She closed her eyes briefly and then opened them. "I don't think your leg bothers you one little bit."

"Not bad," he said approvingly. "The injury itself was minor. The cast is more of a precaution—it actually comes off tomorrow." He gave her an unabashed grin. "After tonight, you can get some sleep."

Somehow, Hannah doubted it. Just knowing he was in the apartment upstairs was enough to keep her awake at night.

"I think the whole purpose of this exercise is so that *you* can get some sleep," she reminded him. "Before we start, you'll need to remove any jewelry." She looked pointedly at the slender black chain around his neck, even as she slipped her bangles from around her wrist and removed her earrings.

Obediently, Ransom reached up and removed his dog tags. "I'm not sure these qualify as jewelry, but here you go." He dropped the tags into her waiting palm, then unfastened his watch and added that, as well. Before she realized his intent, he caught her wrist, pulling her empty hand back toward him and capturing her fingers in his. "No rings?"

"Ah, no," she said, as he rubbed a finger over the indent where a ring had once been.

"But there was a ring here, once." It was a statement, not a question.

"I usually wear my grandmother's ring on that finger, but the stone loosened," Hannah explained. "I actually need to find a jeweler to repair it."

"There's one in Fayetteville that does reputable work. I'll get his number for you."

"Thanks," she said, pulling her hand free. "I'd appreciate that."

As she carefully placed the jewelry and Ransom's necklace on the windowsill, she surreptitiously peeked at the inscription on the flat disks. *BENNETT, RANSOM J.* Beneath that, there was a series of numbers, then his blood type, *A POS,* and his social security number.

Hannah knew there were several military bases close to Cliftondale, and she wondered which branch of the service he belonged to. She could definitely see him being part of some elite unit. He had that kind of aura: indestructible. He also had a body that had been honed to near perfection by rigorous activity. She'd be willing to bet he looked amazing in a uniform.

"Aren't I supposed to take my clothes off, or something?"

Startled back to reality by the amusement in his voice, Hannah turned quickly from her contemplation of his dog tags and his physique.

Her pulse quickened at the image his words conjured up, but she forced herself to smile benignly. "No clothing removal necessary. This is Reiki, not massage. You're fine the way you are."

"Too bad," he murmured.

Hannah ignored his softly murmured comment, even while she silently agreed. The urge to run her hands all over this man was almost overwhelming. Just the sight of him lying on the table, big and muscular and undeniably male, was enough to derail her concentration.

"Stop talking." Unable to resist, she laid a finger across his lips. "Just relax." Beneath her fingertip, his lip curved, and Hannah snatched her hand back.

"So, how long have you been doing this?"

His voice was warm and smoky and Hannah realized she enjoyed listening to him speak.

"I've been interested in Reiki since I was a teenager," she said carefully. "Ever since I discovered—"

She broke off abruptly.

"After you figured out you had a talent for treating pain? I bet that went over like a lead balloon."

His perception took her by surprise. She'd been fourteen when she'd discovered she could actually feel another person's pain, and also alleviate it by laying her hands on that person.

Even knowing her aunt Elle had the same abilities, the knowledge had completely freaked her out. She'd gone to her parents, expecting some kind of assurance or understanding, but instead they'd sat her down and listed all the reasons she should ignore her gift, citing Aunt Elle's experience with the faith ministry as a perfect example.

After that, Hannah hadn't shared any of her healing experiences with them.

"It wasn't an easy time," she admitted. "My folks have never been comfortable with my ability. Hands-on healing sort of runs in the family, and we, um, have a family member who had a bad experience with it. My *gift* was the big, white elephant sitting in the middle of the living room that everyone ignored."

"That must have been rough."

"Well, I was lucky. My aunt understood what I was going through, and steered me toward holistic healing." She tried to ignore how completely tempting Ransom looked, stretched out on her massage table. "It's been a good career choice for me."

"Is that what you call it? A career?"

"Jeez." Hannah laughed. "You ask a lot of questions."

He shrugged. "Hey, I'm putting myself in your hands. Literally. I just want to make sure you're qualified to do this."

"I studied Reiki and spiritual wellness at a healing institute in California. If you'd like, I can show you my certifications."

"Is that an invitation?" There was no mistaking the teasing tone of his voice. "Sort of like, *wanna come up and see my etchings?*"

Yes.

With a sense of shock, Hannah realized she wouldn't be at all averse to showing Ransom her etchings, and a whole lot more. The guy was maleness personified, and just being this close to him was doing strange things to her pulse, never mind her imagination.

"If you really want to see them, I'll dig them out. They're in a box somewhere."

"Maybe later." His eyes slid over her, and his voice dropped an octave. "Right now, why don't you stop talking and start doing."

His voice was so full of meaning that Hannah looked sharply at him, wondering if she'd misunderstood him. But he'd closed his eyes, and although a small smile curved his lips, his face was a portrait of innocence.

"First, I'm going to clear the room of negative energy," she said, modulating her voice to a low, soothing tone. "Are you comfortable?"

"You bet."

Conscious of him watching her, she drew in a deep breath and quickly cleansed the room by staring at each corner in turn, and blowing energy toward it. "This room is cleansed, purified and ready for Reiki healing today," she intoned solemnly.

Beside her, Ransom made a noise that sounded suspiciously like a stifled snort. Hannah pinioned him with what she hoped was a severe look, but he had closed his eyes. For a moment, she was transfixed by the sight of him. He appeared utterly relaxed, as if he was sleeping. Only the slight twitch at one corner of his mouth gave him away. It wasn't until he cracked an eyelid and peered up at her that she gave herself a mental shake and forced herself to stop ogling him.

"I'm going to cleanse your aura before we start." Refusing to be intimidated by his skeptical expression, Hannah positioned her hands just above his head and then swept them slowly down his body to his feet. "This will help you absorb energy," she said, repeating the motion once more.

"Uh-huh."

Hannah heard the cynicism in his voice, but ignored it. "We come together for the highest level of Reiki healing today," she said.

The familiar words helped to center her. After positioning her chair at the end of the table near Ransom's head, she sat down and placed her hands over his eyes, with her thumbs on either side of his nose. Dull pain throbbed briefly behind her eyes when she touched him, but this time she was ready for it. The ache vanished as quickly as it had appeared. Beneath her fingers, his skin was warm and his eyelashes feathered against her palms.

"I'm going to focus on your headaches," she told him. "Just relax. You may experience some warmth or tingling, and you may have an emotional response to the treatment, but it's all normal."

"Sure."

He was anything but relaxed. Outwardly, he appeared loose-limbed and comfortable, but Hannah could sense the tension in him. Closing her eyes, she consciously opened herself to allow energy to flow through her and into Ransom. Almost immediately, her hands grew warm and a tingling sensation spread upward from her fingertips.

Images and colors swam through her mind, most of them dark and disturbing. The imagery was so disquieting and the energy associated with it so negative, that it was all she could do not to end the session immediately. Instead, she kept her hands over his eyes until the darkness subsided and the chaotic imagery became calmer, more peaceful.

"You doing okay?" She kept her voice soft.

"Yeah." His voice was thick. "It feels…strange."

Hannah smiled. "In a good way, though, right?"

"Hmm. Not sure."

Removing her hands from where they rested on his face, she slid them beneath his head, spearing her fingers through the rough silk of his hair to cup his scalp. "How's this?"

"Fantastic." He didn't open his eyes, and there was no denying the sincerity in his voice.

Hannah continued the session, repositioning her hands on different areas of his body until she sensed he had absorbed as much energy as possible. She tried not to think about the firm ridges of muscle that layered his abdomen, or how hot his bare thighs felt beneath her fingers.

She let instinct take over, moving her hands to those parts of his body where she sensed an excess of negative energy. When she placed her hand over his left knee, new images swirled through her mind. The emotions that accompanied them were stark and raw, filled with both anguish and fury.

"Did you have family problems when you were a teenager?" she asked.

He stiffened for an instant then shrugged. "Maybe. What teenager doesn't? Why?"

"I sense so much negative energy in this joint." Hannah began working her thumbs into the tight muscles around the knee. "You're holding all that energy right *here*."

"Ahh." Ransom made a deep groaning sound of pain-pleasure. "Damn."

"You need to let it go," she said. "Whatever happened, it's in your past and you need to release it."

He made a snorting sound of disgust. "Yeah, okay. Tell me how you forget when your own mother walks out on you and your little brother, and never looks back."

Hannah's heart constricted at the bitterness in his voice. "Is that what happened? She left you?"

"She didn't leave us—she obliterated us. From her memory, from her life."

"Us. As in…you, your brother and your dad?" She continued to work her hands into his hard muscles.

"He was a career army guy. We managed."

"How old were you?"

"Eleven."

Hannah kept her hands over his knee joint for several long moments, until she felt some of the negative energy abate. She tried to imagine Ransom as a little boy. Had he believed his mother would come back? How long had he held on to that hope before he'd realized she really had abandoned him? That kind of childhood trauma would leave deep, lasting scars.

"Don't look so worried," he said wryly, accurately reading her thoughts. "The army shrink has assured me that while it was a traumatic experience, I coped with it well. I might even have a chance at a normal relationship someday."

While his humor was self-deprecating, Hannah studied his face and realized he wasn't joking.

"Do you worry about that?" she asked quietly. "About not being able to trust a woman with your heart?"

He made a sound that was part laugh and part groan. "Shit. This was not what I came down here for. Darlin', stick to what you *are* good at, and leave the psychoanalysis to the professionals."

Far from being offended, Hannah recognized that she'd hit a little too close to home for his comfort. She suspected a guy like Ransom Bennett—a career military man—might not be entirely in touch with his feelings. He probably squelched any emotions by going out and blowing something up.

"Are your folks still alive?"

"And doing quite well, thank you."

The tone of his voice said clearly he wasn't interested in answering any more questions. He watched her through hooded eyes. His face was etched with the physical pain he endured from his migraines, but there was cynicism there, too. She couldn't imagine what he'd gone through as a kid, couldn't imagine what it must have been like for him to have his mother vanish from his life. It was unthinkable.

In her world, parents didn't leave their children. They might ignore them, or criticize them for not living up to their expectations, but they didn't abandon them completely.

But she didn't want to think about that, either.

"I think we're through," she said. When Ransom tried to rise, she pushed him gently back with a hand on his chest. "Not so fast. I still need to do another aura cleansing."

"How do you know it's dirty?" His voice dropped an octave, became husky and suggestive. "Can you read my mind?"

Hannah's breath caught. She stood by the table, momentarily paralyzed. She understood that for a moment there, they'd gotten a little too serious. At least for his comfort. He probably regretted sharing that personal bit of information about his mother, and now he was trying to leverage the playing field again, make it seem like it was no big deal.

He was teasing her, she decided, but the expression in his darkly blue eyes was anything but joking. The man from the previous night had returned, and his effect on her was even more potent than it had been in the predawn hours. Without the dulling effects of alcohol and pain meds, the heat in his gaze was intoxicating.

Be professional. Be professional.

The words played through her head like a mantra. She forced herself to ignore the answering heat that flamed to life between her thighs and caused her breasts to tighten. Had he truly had dirty thoughts of her? The very idea was enough to make her go damp, but no matter how irresistible he might be, she wouldn't cross that line. He was here for treatments, and nobody would ever again accuse her of selling sex out of her shop. Although, she mused, she and Ransom weren't actually in her shop and, technically, he wasn't even a client. Sex in exchange for Reiki treatments could be considered an even exchange of services. Or an exchange of energy.

Hannah had an insane urge to giggle, and it was enough to snap her out of the fantasy. She swept her hands over the length of his body. "It's not a matter of being clean or dirty," she explained, but couldn't bring herself to meet his gaze. "This will help to seal in the energy you've just absorbed, and also prevent any negative energy from finding its way in."

"Uh-huh."

Hannah stood back, hands on her hips, exasperated by his tone. She considered him for a moment, and then turned to scoop his dog tags and watch from the windowsill. "You don't believe any of this, do you?" she asked as she held out his belongings.

Ransom pushed himself to a sitting position and wordlessly took the items from her. He fastened the watch around his wrist, and then, as he slid his tags around his neck, he experimentally turned his head from side to side, wincing. When he spoke, his voice was gravelly, and she might have imagined the sexual undertone in his voice scant seconds earlier.

"I'll tell you what. When I walked through your door, my head hurt. It wasn't bad, more like a dull ache. But right now, I feel like my skull is going to explode. So you tell me why I should believe in your energy healing." He turned to her, letting Hannah see the truth in his words.

"It's only temporary," she said soothingly. "Sometimes Reiki makes the symptoms stronger before they subside."

"Then maybe it's not Reiki I need." He didn't elaborate, just continued to watch her in a way that made her want to squirm.

She knew what he wanted, she just wasn't sure she could give him the relief he needed. Despite some of the disturbing imagery she'd experienced during the treatment, the Reiki session had left her feeling incredibly peaceful, and as selfish as it was, she was reluctant to dispel that.

His steady regard unnerved her.

"Okay, fine," she relented. "I'll do what I can, but I have to warn you, it's only a temporary fix. My touch isn't as powerful or as long-lasting as the Reiki."

"Just touch me." It wasn't a request, it was a command.

Heat swamped her midsection and her heart began to thud hard. Oh, she wanted to touch him all right, but not in the way he meant. Reluctantly, she moved to stand directly in front of him. Ransom opened his knees to give her better access, and she stepped between them so that his lean thighs bracketed her hips.

Her breathing quickened. He was so close that she could see the fine pores of his skin. He moistened his lips, and in that instant, Hannah had a nearly overwhelming urge to cover his mouth with her own, to slide her palms along the hard, muscled length of his bare thighs and run her hands over the smooth skin beneath his T-shirt. She could smell him, a mixture of soap and shampoo and something else that was uniquely him. The scent was exhilarating.

She swallowed hard and swiped her damp hands across the seat of her skirt. Then, drawing in several shallow breaths, like a runner on her mark, she lifted her hands toward his face. For just an instant, their eyes locked and her hands hovered in the air between them. Ransom's pupils dilated, turning his irises almost completely black, and Hannah felt something pass between them, something tight and needful. Disconcerted, she took a jerky step backward.

"Easy," Ransom said, and his hands went to her waist to steady her. The heat of his hands warmed her through the thin fabric of her top.

"Sorry." She dragged her gaze away from his. Hesitating only briefly, Hannah placed her hands on either side of his face, covering his temples with her fingers. She heard Ransom's sharply indrawn breath as pain lashed through her skull, fierce and insistent, before slowly fading to a dull ache. He hadn't removed his hands from her waist and she was acutely conscious of their heat, penetrating the thin fabric of her cotton shirt and warming the flesh beneath.

Hannah closed her eyes and concentrated, gently massaging his temples with her fingertips. This wasn't Reiki. Her ability to sense pain in others had nothing to do with the energy of the universe. Neither did her ability to soothe that pain. She wasn't quite sure where the gift came from, or how it worked. Sometimes, it didn't. There had been numerous times when she'd laid hands on somebody in an attempt to relieve their discomfort, and nothing happened.

But when it did work...the sensation was indescribable.

Sometimes she felt as if she were in a centrifuge ride at a carnival, being spun around so hard that she could no longer move, could no longer breathe. At the precise moment when she thought she might actually pass out, the center of her spinning world would suddenly come into sharp relief and she could *see* the person's pain. If she concentrated hard enough, the area would materialize in her mind and then slowly dissipate as she focused on it.

She didn't employ her unique skill very often. The process completely sapped her strength and left her queasy. Now she focused on Ransom's pain, visualizing it as a dark splotch that she slowly erased, beginning at the edges and working her way toward the middle. She almost made it to the center, but before she could eliminate the dark image completely, a wave of nausea overcame her.

"I'm sorry," she gasped, snatching her hands away from Ransom. She bent over and sucked in several deep breaths, willing her stomach to stay put. "I can't—"

To her utter mortification, Ransom was on his feet and lifting her onto the massage table. Before she could protest, he pushed her head firmly down between her knees.

"Deep breaths," he ordered. "Slowly...in, then out...in...out."

Hannah groaned. "I hate when this happens."

His hand was at the back of her head, holding it down, but his fingers massaged her scalp. "Just breathe."

There was a momentary silence, broken only by the soft music that played in the background. Finally, Hannah waved him away. "It's okay, I'm feeling better."

He withdrew his hand, and Hannah sat up. She felt slightly dizzy, as if she'd stood up too fast, but the nausea had at least subsided. She pushed her hair back from her face, only to find him standing directly in front of her.

Disconcerted by his nearness, she strove for a light tone. "Wow. That was a doozy."

She was unprepared when he tilted her face up with one hand, while his other hand encircled her wrist. His fingers were warm and callused. Startled, Hannah's first instinct was to twist away, but he'd have none of it.

"Take it easy," he commanded quietly. "I just want to make sure you're okay."

"I'm fine. How's your headache?" she asked in a desperate attempt to distract him from touching her. His fingers were warm against her skin and she had only to turn her cheek to press it into his palm. She brought her focus back to his face, but he'd moved his attention to his wristwatch.

"Never mind that. How're you feeling?"

"I already told you, I'm fine. Really. This happens sometimes when I do a hands-on healing."

"Then you should have refused me," he said. His voice sounded rough, like he was a little pissed off.

"Oh, yeah. Right." She made no effort to hide her sarcasm.

He glanced swiftly up at her, his black eyebrows pulled together. "I wouldn't have forced you. You can always say no." He stared at her for a long moment, and it was Hannah who looked away first. "But thank you. The headache is practically gone."

He had two fingers pressed against her pulse, and Hannah realized he was checking her vitals.

"I really am okay," she assured him. "Just a little tired."

"Your pulse is rapid."

Hannah laughed weakly. "What a surprise."

The guy had absolutely no idea how much he affected her.

How would he react if she told him her heart rate was a little frantic because he was touching her?

Ransom released her and gave her a questioning look. "What's so funny?"

"It doesn't matter." She waved her hand dismissively. "So what are you, a medic or something?"

"I have some basic first-aid training."

"Is that required in the military? I mean, you are in the military, right?"

"Yeah," he agreed. "I'm in the military. I'm trained as a medic, but it's not my specialty."

He hadn't stepped back. He still stood too close. Hannah looked at him expectantly.

"What?" he asked.

"So the obvious question is…what *is* your specialty?"

There was no way he could have missed the suggestion in her tone, but his response was formally polite. "I'm with an infantry unit."

Unable to stop herself, Hannah reached out and traced her fingers over his T-shirt, where the word *ARMY* was printed in paint that had faded and cracked from washing.

"So, you're in the army?" She glanced up at his face, and her breath caught. His eyes were locked on hers. There was no formality there now; if anything, the expression on his face was shockingly intimate, as if he knew the direction of her thoughts.

"Yeah," he said quietly. "I work over at Camp Lejeune."

"Oh," she murmured, and her fingers continued to trail across the letters on his shirt, as her gaze drifted over his face and lingered on his mouth. Where the rest of his face was hard angles and chiseled planes, his lips were full and mobile. He had a beautiful mouth, made for kissing.

She wondered how he would react if she stood up and pressed her lips against his. She'd had the urge to do just that since she'd watched him sip tea out of her grandmother's best china. Okay, that wasn't the truth. She'd actually fantasized about kissing him since last night.

"That's good," she finally managed to say, moistening her lips, "because I'm a firm believer in, um, supporting our troops."

"You're a dangerous woman," he said softly, and he cupped her elbows in his big hands and drew her to her feet.

Hannah stared up at him, mesmerized. "Why?"

"Because you make me want to do things I have no damned business doing."

His voice was no more than a husky rasp, scraping gently across Hannah's heightened senses and causing heat to unfurl and blossom between her thighs.

"Like what?" she asked breathlessly, and moved infinitesimally closer to him.

"Like this," he said, and bent his head toward hers.

6

HER LIPS WERE incredibly soft. Ransom sensed her surprise as, for just an instant, she stood stiff and unresponsive. He also knew the second her resistance melted. She made a soft mewling sound of pleasure and suddenly her arms were around him and she was kissing him back, hungrily.

Ransom knew that kissing her was a mistake. A huge, atomic, dumb-ass mistake. He had no business getting involved with this girl. He'd seen the pale band of skin on her finger where a ring had once been. She'd claimed the missing ring was her grandmother's, but even though it was a plausible explanation, he wondered if it was the truth.

He hadn't planned on kissing her, but then she'd looked up at him through her thick lashes, and he'd been trapped in the incredible depths of her blue eyes. He'd thought she was attractive last night, but he hadn't had a true appreciation for the flawless clarity of her skin, or her lush, pink lips. That, combined with the sultriness in her voice, and he was powerless to resist kissing her. Any thoughts of pulling away were buried beneath a steamroller of sensation as he felt her tongue make a tentative exploration of his mouth.

His hands, which were still cupping her elbows, slid to her back, and he pressed her more fully against him, amazed at how delicate she felt in his arms. She scarcely came up to his shoulder, and he had to hunch over a little to reach her. But as small as she was, there was no mistaking that she was every inch a woman.

He slid one hand down over the curve of her bottom, and she responded by pressing her hips against him and spearing her fingers into his hair to hold him captive as she slanted her mouth across his. She wasn't just kissing him, she was devouring him, her soft lips feasting on his as her tongue performed an erotic dance against his own. She made a little noise in the back of her throat, somewhere between a whimper of need and a moan of pleasure, and he was done. It was the most erotic sound he'd ever heard, and caused lust to jackknife through him.

With a groan of defeat, he cupped her fanny in his hands and lifted her so that she sat on the edge of the massage table, her slim legs hooked around the back of his thighs. He dragged his mouth from hers enough to look down at her flushed features. Her eyes were clouded with desire as she pulled his head back down to hers.

"Jesus," he said against her mouth, his voice no more than a ragged whisper. "I could kiss you like this all day."

He felt her smile, and then she slid her hands beneath the hem of his T-shirt. They were silken soft and warm against his bare flesh. "So what's stopping you?"

Her whispered challenge was enough to snap the last of his self-restraint, and with a soft growl of capitulation, he captured her face between his hands and fastened his lips over hers. She tasted heady and delicious and he hadn't exaggerated when he said he could kiss her endlessly. Less than twelve hours earlier, sex had been the last thing on his mind. Right now, it was all he could think about.

How long had it been, anyway? Too long. At least five months. His most recent sexual encounter had occurred shortly before he'd left on his last mission. The woman had been a friend of a buddy, guaranteed to show him a good time without any questions asked, or any expectations for the future.

He could remember her name and her face, but damned if he

could remember what the sex had been like. Just two minutes of kissing Hannah Hartwell had pretty much obliterated any memories of that dispassionate coupling.

She was so responsive, both greedy and giving all at once. Best of all, he could actually focus on the exquisite pleasure of touching her. He was free, at least for the moment, from the excruciating headaches, and he intended to enjoy every second. He took his time, tracing the contours of her lips with his tongue and nibbling at the corners of her mouth, while alternately letting her give him hot, openmouthed kisses that caused heat to spiral through him.

Beneath his shirt, Hannah's palms smoothed across his rib cage and around to his back, where her fingertips pressed into his spine, urging him closer. He slid one hand down the length of her back and lower, to cup her buttocks and pull her right to the edge of the table, where he pressed himself against her center. Hannah made a soft sound of approval and twined her legs around his to draw him closer.

Slow down. *Slow. Down.*

More than anything, Ransom wanted to lay Hannah back on the narrow massage table, peel her clothes from her body, and pay homage to all that pale skin and the secrets now hidden from his sight. But he needed to slow down.

He needed to stop.

He had no business getting involved with this girl, especially knowing he couldn't offer her anything more than a superficial relationship. He'd use her for sex, at least during the short periods he'd be home, and then he'd disappear again, sometimes for long stretches of time, and he wouldn't be able to explain why. It was all part of the Delta Force job description.

He'd accepted the fact that his career would always be shrouded in secrecy, and that even his family would never know exactly what it was that he did for a living. But the thought of lying to Hannah, with her open smile and trusting eyes, made him feel like shit. Not only that, but he had a feeling she'd know when he wasn't being truthful with her. She'd probably jump to conclusions and figure he wasn't interested, which wouldn't come close to the truth.

She deserved better.

Her delicate bone structure and wide eyes put him in mind of a Disney princess, the kind his little niece loved so much. Hannah was the type of girl who'd probably been cherished and spoiled her whole life. She'd probably been raised on fairy tales with happily-ever-afters. He liked to think he wasn't such an asshole as to take advantage of that.

Reluctantly, he dragged his mouth from hers and when she would have protested, he pressed her face gently into his shoulder. He breathed in the clean fragrance of her hair, aware they were both panting heavily, as if they'd sprinted up several flights of stairs.

Ransom sucked in a deep breath, waiting for his heart to regulate itself. He could feel the rapid rise and fall of Hannah's chest against his own. Her hands were still beneath his shirt, and her fingers rubbed slow circles on his skin.

"Why did you stop?" Her voice was muffled against his chest.

Ransom gave a huff of disbelieving laughter. "You're kidding, right? Another five minutes of that, and you'd be naked on this table, with your legs around my back."

Hannah tipped her head back to look at him. Her eyes still looked a little dazed and her lips were moist and ripe from his kisses. She smiled, and Ransom felt something in his chest shift.

"You say that like it's a bad thing. I mean, unless you have something better to do…" She let the sentence trail off meaningfully.

Ransom stared down at her, hardly able to believe what she was offering. "Are you propositioning me?" His voice sounded strangled.

Hannah tucked a loose piece of hair behind her ear and sat up straighter. Her voice sounded a tiny bit defensive. "What if I am?"

Unable to help himself, Ransom started to laugh. The day just kept getting better and better. In fact, it was turning out to be freaking unforgettable. Yep, just when he decided to go all Dudley Do-Right, fate threw temptation squarely in his face.

A frown hitched between Hannah's eyebrows as she watched him struggle to compose himself. After a moment, he stopped laughing, but his shoulders still shook with aftershocks.

"You find it amusing that I should find you attractive?"

The heat in her eyes had dropped several degrees. He'd pissed her off, which hadn't been his intent, but he couldn't believe she was actually suggesting they finish what they'd started.

"Lady," he said, composing himself, "I find it freaking unbelievable."

He saw the steely glint that entered Hannah's eyes, and it should have been his cue to beat feet out of there, but there was no doubt about it; he was a true glutton for punishment. He wanted to see how she'd react.

"Well," she said softly, "maybe I should prove to you just how attractive I find you."

Before Ransom could guess her intent, she bunched his T-shirt in her hands and pushed it up over his stomach, following it with her hands.

"Mmm," she said approvingly, "very nice." Then she leaned forward and very delicately traced the outline of his nipple with her tongue.

Ransom's reaction was instantaneous as his dick leaped to attention and strained against the fabric of his cargo shorts. "Okay," he said, catching hold of her hands and tugging them away. "I think you've proven your point."

She managed to press one last kiss against his heated flesh, scraping him gently with her teeth and causing shivers of sheer sensation to chase down his spine, before he set her away.

"Look," he said, raw desire lending his voice a gravelly quality, "I appreciate what you're doing, but I'm going to have to pass. It's not personal. I just happen to like my women with a little more T & A than you're sporting."

He was lying through his teeth, but there was no way he could let her see just how much he wanted her. He wasn't sure how long his good intentions could hold out if she persisted, and damn it, he was really trying to do the right thing.

He could almost predict how any relationship between them would progress. She'd become attached to him, but wouldn't understand his inability to make a commitment. Eventually, she'd come to resent him. He'd begin sneaking in and out of the house in order to avoid her, only eventually there'd be an ugly confrontation.

Nope, better to just nip it in the bud now, before it really got started.

He'd shifted slightly so that he was no longer pressed against the sweet juncture of her thighs, but all she had to do was look to see how painfully aroused he was. Luckily, she didn't. Instead, she stared at him, appalled.

"T & A? Are you referring to my...my feminine attributes?"

"Yeah, actually, I am." He forced himself to look unabashed.

"Is that how you view all women, Mr. Bennett? As the sum total of their tits and ass?"

"Well, let's not forget the all-important—"

"Stop!" Hannah clapped her hands over her ears.

If anything, her reaction to his crudeness only confirmed Ransom's belief that she was a woman he'd do best to stay away from. Her sensibilities were just a little too refined for a guy like him. She might not realize it, but he was doing her a favor by turning her down.

When it became clear he wasn't going to finish his sentence, she lowered her hands. "Well, Mr. Bennett, I guess we're through."

"Yeah, I guess we are."

He didn't bother to tell her that in his world, he was referred to as Chief Bennett, or Ransom. He doubted she'd give a rat's ass what he was called; at this point, she probably had a few choice names of her own to recommend.

Ransom turned away from her, covertly adjusting himself to a less conspicuous degree before he stepped away from the table, telling himself he was the biggest ass on the face of the planet. Any other red-blooded male would have taken what she'd so sweetly offered.

Leave it to him to do the right thing.

He turned just in time to see Hannah scoot off the edge of the massage table, her skirt shimmying up to reveal slender, toned thighs. He nearly groaned aloud at his own idiocy. Right now, he could have those gorgeous legs wrapped around his waist as he drove himself into her welcoming heat.

He needed to get out of her apartment before he did something supremely stupid, like admit that he actually found her completely hot.

Too hot.

So hot, in fact, that he was in danger of going against his better judgment and showing her just how much they *weren't* through. Swearing softly, he made a beeline for the door.

"So I'll see you later on?"

For a millisecond, Ransom actually thought she'd read his mind. He stopped but didn't turn around.

"For what?"

Her voice came from directly behind him. "You weren't thinking of welshing on our deal, were you?" She swished past him, out of the little room and back into the living area.

Ransom followed her, his eyes riveted on the gentle swing of her bottom beneath the sea-colored skirt. Sunlight glinted on the metallic disks stitched into the fabric and flung glittering, iridescent patterns against the wall. Out of sheer habit, he put up a hand to protect his eyes from the brightness of the living room, but realized his headache really had vanished. The light didn't bother him the way it had when he'd first entered her apartment.

"Ah," he said, finally understanding. "Our deal. The one where you treat my headaches and I help you fix up your shop."

Hannah stood with her hand on the doorknob, clearly anxious to be rid of him. "Yes, *that* deal. Unless you'd prefer to change the terms…"

Her voice trailed off, and the suggestive expression in her eyes was enough to send his blood surging to a certain part of his anatomy. He couldn't believe she was still interested in him that way, or that he was still going to be a dumb-ass and pretend to misunderstand her.

"I wasn't sure you'd still want me hanging around," he said carefully. Despite the fact that he knew he should stay away from Hannah Hartwell, there wasn't a snowball's chance in hell he'd turn her down. He just couldn't quite believe she still wanted him to help her. "I mean, the migraine is gone."

"Trust me," she said, opening the door and standing back, "by this time tomorrow, you're going to be begging me to touch you again." A small smile curved her lips.

Her words caused Ransom's imagination to soar. The worst part was, he knew she was right. Just not for the reasons she'd implied.

"We'll see," he said. "Thanks again for—"

Hell.

What was he supposed to say? *Thank you for touching me? You really turned me on?* As it was, he'd be walking around with a serious woody for the rest of the day.

"Thanks for everything," he finished lamely.

Smooth. Real smooth.

"Don't forget to sweep that floor before you walk around barefoot again," he reminded her, and stepped into the hallway.

"Oh, wait!" She laid a hand on his arm, halting him. "That reminds me…there was a man in the house next door."

Ransom arched an eyebrow. "Okay."

He watched with interest as her cheeks pinkened. "He was watching me through binoculars. I saw him. He was in an upstairs window, and I was in the kitchen. That's what made me drop the teacup."

Ransom felt his gut tighten. "I'll take care of it. He won't bother you again."

"Who is he?"

Ransom rubbed a hand across the back of his neck. He'd moved into the second-floor apartment above Hannah's four years ago, and although he hadn't made any friends in the neighborhood, he'd made a point of learning who his neighbors were. He'd chosen the area because there were several military families and a couple of single enlisted guys who also lived on the street. They didn't mind keeping an eye on his apartment when he deployed. He'd checked out the guy in the house next door and, despite his odd behavior, knew he wasn't a threat.

"His name is Mike Howard. He's a Vietnam veteran. He's lived there for years, but he has this thing about strangers…"

Hannah's face lost a little of its rosy hue. "What do you mean, a *thing?*"

Ransom could tell by the expression on her face that she was having lurid images of some deranged vet experiencing a flashback and mistaking *her* for the enemy.

"He's harmless," he assured her. "Mike was a Tunnel Rat during the war. The army gave him the Silver Star for bravery, but his hero days are long past. He hardly ever leaves his house, but he likes to watch what's going on in the neighborhood."

"Oh."

"Like I said, he's harmless, but I'll have a word with him about the binoculars. He shouldn't watch you through your windows."

"I'd appreciate it. Thanks."

She closed the door, and Ransom started upstairs.

He could protect Hannah from Mike Howard, but who would protect her from him?

7

IT WAS NEARLY ten o'clock that night when an abrupt knock sounded at her apartment door. Startled, Hannah leaped to her feet, scattering the papers she'd spread out on the sofa around her. Her laptop was open on the coffee table, where she'd been doing some research on brain injuries. She didn't know how Ransom had been injured, and wondered if it was combat related.

Even from the little bit she knew of him, Ransom showed all the classic signs of a mild brain injury: trouble sleeping, migraines, restlessness. But from what she'd read, it sure as heck didn't seem like the army had a good handle on how to treat the injured men. She didn't know if he was seeing a doctor, but he struck her as the type who wouldn't want anyone to know he was suffering.

He'd want everyone to believe he was A-okay, fit for function. She could almost imagine his reaction if she suggested he might be brain damaged: he'd just flat out scratch her off his dance card. And wouldn't that be a shame?

She'd been so immersed in reading the article that the knock on her door actually frightened her, and her first thought was that Sully had found her. Her gaze flew desperately to the dead bolt as she realized she hadn't locked the door.

"Hannah, it's me."

There was no mistaking the deep, smoky quality of that voice. Her shoulders sagged in relief…before nervous anticipation twisted her stomach. She'd thought of little else but Ransom

Bennett since he'd left earlier that day. If she closed her eyes, she could still feel his body pressed against her own, breathe in the scent of him, and taste his mouth on hers. She tried to focus on the disparaging remarks he'd made about her body. Instead, all she could think about was how hard he'd been, and how he'd kissed her as if his very existence depended on it. The words coming out of his mouth might have said she wasn't his type, but his body had been singing an entirely different tune.

Initially, she'd been insulted by his crude reference to her feminine attributes—or her apparent lack of them—but her indignation hadn't lasted very long. In retrospect, after analyzing both his words and his behavior, she'd realized he'd been totally turned on by her. He'd wanted her but, for some reason, didn't believe he should act on his desires. The knowledge was both thrilling and frustrating.

She could guess why he was at her door at this hour, and it wasn't because he'd had a change of mind and wanted to take her up on her offer. She'd bet money on the fact that his headache had returned and he needed a quick fix in order to sleep. Since reading the article about brain injuries, Hannah was more convinced than ever that he needed her help. His kind of hurt couldn't be cured by doctors alone. His injury went deeper than tissue and bone; his spirit needed to heal as much as his body did.

She told herself she didn't feel the slightest flutter of anticipation at the thought of putting her hands on Ransom Bennett again.

But when she opened the door, she knew she was a liar. Her entire body responded to the sight of him as he leaned negligently against the doorjamb. He looked faintly piratical with the scar slashing across his forehead and a day's growth of whiskers shadowing his lean jaw. But his eyes were clear and he didn't look like a man in pain.

"Hey," she said in greeting, hoping her voice didn't betray her pleasure at seeing him. Or her hope that maybe he really *was* here for something other than a Reiki treatment. While he'd made it clear she wasn't his type, each time she saw him, she became more convinced that he might be hers. "And here I thought I had the monopoly on late-night visits."

He didn't answer. Instead, his eyes drifted over her body, reminding Hannah that she wore nothing more than a bright yellow sports bra and a minuscule pair of silky running shorts, folded down at the waistband. Her standard nightwear on hot, sticky nights. At least when she was alone.

But with his dark eyes on her, it was all she could do not to cross her arms over her bare midriff. She couldn't recall the last time she'd been so aware of herself as a woman.

"Very nice." His eyes gleamed as he took in the tiny crescent moon that dangled in her navel, its jeweled surface glinting in the light.

"Thanks." She stood back and opened the door wider. "Do you want to come in?"

"Ah, no. I wanted to let you know that I had a word with Mike Howard." When she didn't answer, he clarified. "The guy with the binoculars."

"Oh! Yes. *Him.*" She tipped her head as she considered Ransom, wondering how *that* had gone. "And?"

"He, ah, thinks you're part of a government conspiracy to kidnap him and force him back into military service."

"What?"

Ransom shrugged. "He's off his meds. I assured him that's not the case, and then called the V.A. to send somebody out to check on him."

Hannah clapped a hand to her forehead. "Oh, my God. He thinks I'm one of those enemy combatants! He's probably over there right now, plotting ways to *eliminate* me."

"Yeah, well, he's pretty convinced you're some kind of covert operative, designed to dazzle him with your beauty and make him go willingly with you wherever you want." He had the audacity to grin. "I pretty much couldn't convince him otherwise."

Images of herself, clad in an Emma Peel black leather catsuit, flashed through her mind. Groaning, she scrubbed her hands over her face before steepling her fingers in front of her mouth. "So what do I do?"

"Nothing." But his gaze dropped down the length of her body, lingering on the pale skin of her bare abdomen before leisurely studying her legs. "Although I might be inclined to cover up a bit more, if I were you. Maybe if there's less exposed flesh to bedazzle him, he won't think you're a spy sent to seduce him."

"Cover up?" Hannah gaped at him. "You're kidding, right? In case you haven't noticed, it's about a gazillion degrees outside. I am *not* covering up. Jeez."

"Yeah, I didn't think you'd go for that. Do yourself a favor, though, and at least buy some shades, okay? You can't blame the guy for watching through binoculars, not when you prance around without any clothes on."

"He said that?" Hannah looked at Ransom in horror. It was true; she *did* have a habit of walking naked from the bedroom to the bathroom, but she'd never guessed she had an audience.

"Something to that effect. Maybe with a little more description."

His words, combined with the heated slide of his eyes across her body, caused warmth to unfurl low in Hannah's abdomen. God, he really was gorgeous, especially when his lips curved in a lazy smile, the way they were doing right now. It was enough for her to almost forget that he'd pretended he didn't find her attractive.

"Okay. Well, thanks and have a good night. Off to get dressed for bed…in the dark…so nobody sees me." She made to shut the door, but he forestalled her with one hand against it.

"Actually, there's another reason I stopped by. I was hoping you could open up the shop and show me what you need done."

Hannah stared at him. *"Now?"*

He shrugged. "Why not?"

"Because it's ten o'clock at night, that's why."

"This won't take long. I just want to get an idea of what materials you'll need. I'll pick them up first thing in the morning and get started."

Hannah narrowed her eyes at him. "Are you doing this because I accused you of welshing?"

"Absolutely. Not." He grinned at her. "C'mon, darlin'. Let's go take a look. Opening day will be here before you know it."

It was the truth. She felt overwhelmed by the sheer enormity of what still needed to be done before the shop could be considered ready for the public. And she had already advertised the opening date in the local paper. She should be grateful for Ransom's help.

"Okay," she finally relented. "Wait here. I just need to grab the keys."

She left Ransom in the doorway and hurried into her bedroom to retrieve the keys from her nightstand. She was gone less than a minute, but when she came back into the living room, it was to find Ransom collecting her scattered papers from the floor around the sofa. As he bent down to scoop the papers together, his eyes were on her laptop, swiftly scanning the contents of the Web page.

"Oh, please," she protested, "you don't need to do that." She stepped forward to take the loose papers from him, and snapped the laptop shut.

"Just trying to be helpful," he said.

Hannah eyed him anxiously as she turned the papers facedown on the kitchen counter. Maybe he hadn't had enough time to scan the article and figure out she'd been reading up on brain injuries. Maybe, if she was lucky, he didn't associate that terminology with himself, and believed she was educating herself as part of her Reiki practice. Yeah, right. And maybe he was a complete simpleton, too.

"I'll, um, open the shop for you," she mumbled.

He followed her into the hallway and outside onto the sidewalk. The night air was soft and sultry and tinged with the scent of the ocean. The salty fragrance never failed to soothe Hannah. There were times when she could close her eyes and almost convince herself that she was still in New England.

"Nice sign," Ransom commented from behind her.

She paused for a moment at the door to the shop and glanced at the large banner she'd hung in the enormous picture window overlooking the street. Even by the faint light of the nearby streetlamp, the words were easily discernible: *Body & Soul—Spiritual Wellness Shop—Grand Opening Sep 21*. She'd painted it herself, in bold colors, and it glowed eerily against the backdrop of darkness.

"Thanks." He'd come to stand directly behind her as she fitted the key to the lock, and she could sense his presence as surely as if he had touched her. She pushed the door open and stepped into the dark interior of the shop, groping for the light switch. When she found it, she had to blink at the sudden flood of fluorescence.

"Maybe the first thing you should do is invest in some different lighting," Ransom commented, as she closed the door behind them. "This isn't exactly conducive to relaxation."

"It's on my list," she assured him, and bent over to push a cardboard box aside. "Along with about a million other things."

Hannah looked around at the small room. The hardwood floors were in good shape, and gleamed under the garish light. Several comfortable chairs stood in front of the windows, and a small reception counter faced the street. A glass case stood against another wall, where she intended to display her crystals and jewelry. It fit well into the corner, and she was glad that she hadn't left it behind.

She'd paid a small fortune to have a moving company from New York transport the furniture and supplies from her former

shop in South Boston, to Cliftondale. The movers hadn't asked
any questions, either, like why she needed them to come at the
crack of dawn on a Sunday morning, when most of the neighborhood was still asleep, or why she insisted they park their
moving truck in the narrow alley behind her building, rather
than out front on the main street.

It hadn't taken them long to load her things into the cargo
van; she'd spent most of that week covertly boxing up her belongings and moving them toward the back entrance of the
shop. Forty minutes, that's all it had taken. Forty minutes of
sheer terror, when she'd expected Sully to burst through the
front door of the dark shop and confront her. Forty minutes
while her best friend, Maureen, kept Sully's watchdog occupied
in the backseat of his Hummer. Forty minutes to disappear and
make a new start.

After the moving van had left, lumbering slowly out of the
back alley to follow an indirect route to the expressway, Hannah
had slung a single bag over her shoulder and walked to North
Station, where she'd bought an Amtrak ticket to freedom.

She'd paid cash for everything and hadn't told anyone where
she was going, not even Maureen. Not even her family, not that
she thought they'd be overly concerned. They'd no doubt be
relieved just to have her out of their hair. It was embarrassing to
have a daughter accused of selling sex out of her shop, even if
the charges had been dropped.

The judge had made it clear he thought the case was ludicrous,
and a waste of both his time and taxpayers' money. His words to
Sully had been severe, and Hannah hadn't missed how the officer's face had turned red with fury and embarrassment. Hannah
knew Sully had felt both humiliated and cheated, and it would
only be a matter of time before he paid her another visit. That
was when she'd made the decision to leave Boston for good.

Eventually, she'd contact Maureen and let her know she was

settled, but not until she could be assured that Sully wouldn't come after her.

"So where do we start?"

Ransom's words startled her out of her reverie, bringing her back to the present and to the little shop that represented her new life. Swiping a hand across her eyes, she forced herself to think about the task at hand.

"Well, I bought this ceiling fan." She nudged a box with her foot. "But I have no idea how to assemble or install it."

"No problem."

She gestured to the room around them. "This will be a combination waiting area and New Age store, where customers will be able to buy everything from books and music, to crystals and candles. I'd like to install shelving along these walls, to display the various items I'll sell."

She watched as Ransom pulled a tape measure out of his pocket and took some measurements of the area. "How many shelves, and how deep?" he asked.

"Well, most of the items that I sell are fairly small," Hannah said thoughtfully, considering the products that would be on display. "I think if the shelving is ten inches deep, that'll be great."

Ransom tucked the tape measure into his back pocket. "Done." He surveyed the room, taking in the large glass display case and the cardboard boxes stacked against the wall. "So I think it's a fair assumption to say this isn't your first shop. Where were you located before?"

Hannah stilled. "What makes you think this isn't my first shop?"

Ransom arched an eyebrow. "Darlin', anyone can see you've brought a full truckload of inventory with you."

He pointed to the sign that she'd leaned up against the reception counter. Constructed of heavy wood and painted a bright blue, it was designed to hang over a doorway. Fancy gold lettering read *Body & Soul—Spiritual Wellness & Healing*.

"See those iron brackets on the top of the sign?" He indicated the fasteners where the sign had once hung from an iron arm. "They've seen some wear, which tells me this sign has hung over a storefront before."

"Excellent deduction, Sherlock," she said wryly.

"Was it in Boston?"

"Was what in Boston?" She couldn't prevent the buzzing sensation in her ears, or how his question caused her heart rate to accelerate. She told herself she had nothing to hide; she'd been acquitted of any wrongdoing. But she couldn't meet his eyes. He was too perceptive by far.

"Your shop." His voice was tolerantly amused. "Did you have a shop in Boston?"

"Maybe I bought the sign off eBay. Do you know what it costs to have a custom-made sign made? They're not cheap." Heart hammering, she turned and walked around the reception desk and opened a door to a small hallway. "Let me show you the rest of the shop."

She didn't look to see if Ransom followed her, too afraid of the expression she'd see on his face. Clearly, he wanted to know more about where she'd come from, but she didn't know him well enough to share that information.

At least not yet.

Maybe she would, eventually, but she was still too traumatized and embarrassed by the events in Boston to want to talk about them with anyone, never mind a virtual stranger.

To her immense relief, Ransom didn't press the issue, but she was aware of his eyes on her as he followed her into the hallway.

"There's a small bathroom in here," she said, flipping on the light and glancing around the tiny chamber. "It's not great, but it's clean and functional. I'll add some decorative touches and it'll be fine."

She crossed the hallway and opened a second door. This room

was empty and dark, except for the light that spilled in from the reception area. "This is where I'll do my treatments," she told Ransom. "The carpeting isn't bad, but I'd like to pull it up to reveal the hardwood beneath."

Bending down, Ransom peeled back a corner of the rug near the door and inspected the boards beneath. "That should work. The flooring looks to be in good shape. What else?"

"The walls need to be painted." She indicated the gallon can of paint and assorted rollers near the door. "I've bought all the supplies, but I need to buy a ladder before I can get started. I'd also like some more shelving in here, mostly to store fresh blankets and sheets, and I need somewhere to put my music."

A slight frown drew Ransom's eyebrows together, but he didn't say anything.

"What's wrong?" she asked.

He turned to look at her, and even in the indistinct lighting, there was no mistaking the heat in his eyes. It was enough to steal her breath. His voice was low and gruff. "Do you think it's safe for you to be back here, alone with a client?"

Hannah smiled at him. "Of course. Why wouldn't it be?"

"What if you get a male client who expects…more?"

Hannah stilled. "More *what?*"

She knew exactly what he referred to, and it both amazed and infuriated her that he automatically associated a massage table in a back room with sex. Chiropractors and physicians never had to deal with that kind of stigma, but because she was conducting hands-on energy healing, some people believed she must be performing some kinky sex act with her male clients.

Ransom gave her a tolerant look. "You know damned well what I'm referring to."

Some perverse impulse prompted her to torment him, just a tiny bit.

"Oh," she said, inflecting as much wonder and childish hope

into her voice as she could. "You really think I might have a client who would want sex with me? Despite my inadequate feminine attributes? Golly, jeez!"

"Christ, I never said you were *inadequate,*" he said darkly. "I just happen to know there are a lot of military guys in this area, and not all of them are—"

"As gentlemanly as you?" she finished sweetly. "Don't worry, I can take care of myself."

He made a noise that sounded suspiciously like a snort, and then glanced back toward the reception area. "Do you at least have an assistant?"

"Not yet, but I'm hoping to hire one before the shop opens." She tilted her head and considered him. "I know what you're thinking, but you really *don't* have to worry about me. This isn't a dangerous business."

"Yeah, well, I'd feel a whole lot better if you restricted your clientele to females, and installed a surveillance camera in here." His eyes were traveling the perimeter of the room, as if contemplating the best spot for a video feed.

"If it makes you feel any better, most of my customers *are* women. I only get the occasional man."

"All it takes is one."

He turned his head to look at her, and Hannah found herself unable to look away or even think of something to say to lighten the mood.

"Hannah…"

He took a step toward her. Hannah backed up until she felt the wall behind her, and still he kept coming, until mere inches separated them. A deep breath would bring her breasts into full contact with his chest.

He braced his hands against the wall on either side of her head, imprisoning her. Light shafted through the open door from the reception room, illuminating half of his face and casting the other side in shadow. A muscle worked convulsively in his lean cheek and his eyes were fathomless.

He made no move to touch her, just studied her, feature by feature. He was so close that she could see his pulse throbbing, strong and steady, at the base of his neck. Transfixed by that small disturbance, her fingers traveled upward, to cover the shallow hollow of her own throat. Could he see how rapidly her heart was beating? Could he see how his nearness affected her?

"Hannah," he repeated, softer this time. "Look at you. Do you really think you could stop a man intent on having you? Don't bullshit me. I have a head injury, but I'm *not* brain damaged. Speaking of which…" He trailed off meaningfully.

"No," she finally managed to say, her voice sounding small and strangled. "It won't work—I'm not going to touch you."

"That's okay, darlin'," he rasped, and a ghost of a smile touched his beautiful mouth. His voice slid over her like sun-warmed brandy. "This time, I'm going to touch *you*."

His words caused instant heat to flood her body, and between her legs, she began to pulse. He lowered his head, and she shuddered lightly at the sensation of his lips on the side of her neck. The whiskers on his jaw scratched against the underside of her chin as his mouth closed over her flesh, lifting it and sucking gently. Hannah's hands fisted at her sides, and she closed her eyes against the sight of his broad shoulders poised above her. Her nostrils flared. She could smell him. A clean, male scent of sweat and soap. She realized she had only to turn her face, and her lips would brush along the smooth bulge of his bicep, where his arm was bent against the wall.

He'd stopped sucking on her neck, and was soothing the area with his tongue. She'd have a mark, she was certain. *His mark*. On her flesh.

The thought caused lust to cramp her midsection as she

realized this was what she had wanted since he'd knocked on her door. Since he'd left her apartment earlier that day, actually.

Desire, hot and fierce, lashed through her. Somebody whimpered, a small, desperate sound of need. With a sense of shock, she realized it had come from her. Ransom's hair brushed her chin as he dipped his head and trailed kisses along the line of her collarbone, pausing at the base of her throat, where she knew her pulse beat frantically.

He smiled against her neck, and then he bent lower. He skated his mouth along the smooth skin of her upper chest, and then lower still, over the fabric of her running bra. Hannah's breath was coming faster now. He still had both hands on the wall, but slid them down slightly as he bent toward this new exploration.

Hannah gasped as his mouth closed over her breast beneath the stretchy fabric of the running bra. The combination of heat and moisture caused her nipple to harden. He made a grunting sound of approval and drew harder on the distended nub, and the exquisite sensation shot all the way to her groin. Hannah's limbs loosened, and she pressed her palms hard against the wall to keep from buckling to the floor; to keep from clutching his head and begging him not to stop. She needn't have worried. Ransom wasn't finished.

Dropping to one knee, with his casted leg bent, he released her breast and continued his downward journey, lightly biting her rib cage until he came to the smooth, bare skin of her stomach. Her muscles contracted beneath the heat of his mouth, and when he dipped his tongue into the whorl of her navel, flicking the small jeweled moon that hung there, Hannah moaned.

It was too much, and yet not nearly enough.

"Please," she gasped. The sight of his dark head against her pale abdomen was startling. She wanted to bury her fingers in the rough velvet of his hair and urge him even lower.

As if he could read her very thoughts, his hands moved to

cover hers, trapping them between the wall and his palms. His face dipped lower, until his stubbled jaw brushed against the soft skin of her thighs. Hannah had never before realized just how traitorous her body could be, how her thighs could fall open from no more than the touch of a fevered kiss against the sensitive inner skin.

"That's it," Ransom purred.

His breath was hot and moist, dampening the silken fabric of her running shorts where they covered her. He pressed his mouth against the warm crease where her thigh met her groin, and she whimpered again. Hannah tried to free her hands, but he twined his fingers with hers and held them captive. She was throbbing with need, and when his mouth covered her through the thin fabric of her shorts, she almost wept with relief and frustration.

Ah. Yes. The heat from his breath, combined with the sight of his face buried between her splayed thighs, nearly pushed her over the edge. She was dangerously close to climaxing. He must have sensed how close, because his fingers tightened around hers in silent understanding. His tongue became insistent, shaping her contours through the insubstantial material. She was hot, so hot. And beneath the slippery fabric, slick with desire.

When Ransom flicked his tongue hard against the swollen nub of her clitoris, it was more than she could take. Her head rolled helplessly against the wall as an orgasm racked her body. Only then, as she broke apart, did he release her hands and permit her to slide in a boneless heap to the floor.

Ransom turned to sit with his back against the wall, pulling Hannah with him so that she lay half sprawled against him. For a moment, there was only the sound of her ragged breathing.

"Like I said, darlin'," he murmured, his breath warm against her ear, "all it takes is one."

"That—that wasn't part of the deal," she finally managed to say, pushing herself away from him. Her voice sounded strange, completely unlike her own. She couldn't bring herself to look at him, too embarrassed by the way her body had responded to his touch to meet his eyes. Instead, she took refuge in righteous indignation. "Why is it that men always think they're entitled to sex in exchange for helping a woman?"

When Ransom didn't respond, Hannah rose unsteadily to her feet. Her body still thrummed with sexual aftershocks. "I see how this works." Her voice wobbled, the words tumbling over themselves. "You help me out, and then—and then…"

Despite the bulky cast encasing his lower leg, Ransom rose to his feet in one fluid movement. One second he was sitting on the floor, and the next he was standing over her, his hands curling around her jaw to cradle her face. "And then I bring you to orgasm," he finished softly.

"Oh," Hannah breathed, mesmerized by the expression on his face. "Yes, well…" She cleared her throat. "How, um, nice."

Ransom grinned. "You bet."

8

"I WANT TO KNOW everything there is to know about Ms. Hannah Hartwell. I want to know where she was born, where she was raised, where she went to school and what her GPA was. Hell, I even want to know when she had her first orgasm, and if it was good for her." Ransom pinched the bridge of his nose hard between his thumb and forefinger. Damn, his head hurt. "Actually," he said roughly, looking at the other men in the war room, "forget that last part. I'm not sure I want to know."

The six-man Delta team convened in the secure room at Camp Lejeune every morning, following an hour or more on the shooting range. While Fort Bragg was Delta Force's primary base of operations, it was by no means their only base. Teams of operators were strategically located around the globe, ready to move out at a moment's notice. Camp Lejeune was just one of those locations.

Ransom's phone vibrated at his hip, indicating an incoming text message.

Confirming your 11 a.m. appointment today with Dr. Katz.

Damn. The last thing he wanted to do was meet with the military doc, especially when his headache had taken on the characteristics of a rocket-propelled grenade going off inside his skull. The doctor would take one look at him and declare him medically unfit for combat, sidelining any chance he might have of being part of mission *Formidable Force.*

Absolutely not an option.

Delete.

He glanced around. There were just four operators in the small central control room. Billy Pagan and Denis Tanks had been called back to Fort Bragg to provide their commander with a detailed overview of the pending mission.

Again.

Ransom knew he wasn't the only one frustrated over the Pentagon's reluctance to give them a green light for *Formidable Force.* Each member of the six-man team wanted to be in Afghanistan, hunting the insurgents who had taken two of their best. The weeks of elaborate planning and preparation had made them eager for insertion, despite knowing that failure meant death or capture.

"Christ, Ran, what'd this chick do? Pick you up, then roll you?" Alec Carvotti grinned at the thought of any woman getting the best of Ransom Bennett.

"Nah, with a last name like that she's probably some dancer he met down on the strip," scoffed Jeb Wolfe, without looking up from his computer monitor. Part Shoshone, Jeb had been raised in Las Vegas and was their resident cynic. "Or maybe she's a transvestite."

"Is that what happened, Ran?" One of the men, Conor McCallum, glanced up from where he was examining the latest satellite images from Afghanistan. "Did you cop a feel and find a little more beneath the lady's skirts than you were expecting? Is that it?"

Ransom barely contained a groan. What he'd found hadn't been nearly enough. He'd wanted to drag Hannah's shorts down over her hips, cup her sweet ass in his hands and explore her softness more fully. Her small sounds of pleasure had been a complete turn-on.

He'd only just managed to tamp down his rampant lust and let her leave, but he admitted to himself that his resolve was rapidly deteriorating. He wanted her badly, the consequences be damned. She'd looked at him with such naked desire in her eyes that he'd been tempted to take her right there, on the bare wood floor of her shop. Instead, he had steered her out the front door and had practically sprinted upstairs to his own apartment, where he'd stood under a cool shower and had taken matters into his own hands, so to speak.

His cell phone vibrated again.

Confirm appointment at 11 a.m. today, or consider yourself medically disabled for active duty. Dr. Katz.

Blowing out a hard breath, he punched in a return message.

Appointment confirmed.

He'd just have to fake it as best he could.

Now he looked at each of the men in turn. He'd known them all since before they'd gone through Delta training together at Fort Bragg, and he'd trust each of them with his life. But it was moments like these when he could cheerfully have choked them. His head throbbed, and if he turned too quickly, his vision blurred. He longed for the soothing touch of Hannah's fingers against his temples.

"I can assure you," he growled, pinning Conor with a meaningful look, "that everything beneath the lady's skirts is in perfect working order."

Alec leaned back in his chair and stared at Ransom with something like amazement on his face. His dark eyes gleamed with amusement. "Well, well," he mused, "isn't this something? Ransom Bennett, sidetracked by a woman. Now I'm definitely intrigued."

"Here's a picture I took of her the other day." Ransom slapped a photo of Hannah down on the table next to Alec. "You keep bragging that you're the best Intel in the command, so here's your chance to prove it."

Alec picked up the photo and gave a low whistle. "Hello, Heather Locklear! Not bad, Ran, not bad at all."

The picture had been taken from a vantage point slightly above the subject, from Ransom's second-floor bedroom window. The photo showed a slim woman in shorts and a camisole top standing on a sidewalk. Her blond hair was pulled into a ponytail and her face was turned partially toward the camera, affording a clear shot of her features. She was staring at something and her expression looked startled, even scared.

Conor pushed his chair back from the bank of computer monitors and slid across the floor. He peered at the photo over Alec's shoulder. "Very nice," he allowed after a moment. "What's she afraid of?"

"That's what Alec is going to find out," Ransom said, clapping the other man on the shoulder. "Start with Boston."

Jeb leaned back from his workstation and snatched the photo from Alec's hands. He was normally quick to smile, but now his dark eyebrows drew together as he studied the image. "Tell me this isn't personal."

"Okay," Ransom said easily. "It isn't personal."

"Bullshit. This girl doesn't look like a terrorist, and she sure as hell doesn't look like she has anything to do with *the mission.*" Jeb emphasized the last two words as he tossed the photo back onto the surface of the table with an irritated snap of his wrist. "What's going on, Bennett? For the past six weeks you've been all about *Formidable Force,* and now suddenly you have us investigating some girl? *Christ.*"

Alec shrugged. "You know what they say—if you don't wanna know the answer, don't ask the question."

"I'm asking the question," Ransom said evenly. "And, no, she's not a terrorist. But there's something going on with this girl, and I want to know what it is."

Jeb snorted. "Yeah, like whether or not she has a husband in Boston. Shit, Bennett. You know this goes against—"

"Yeah, yeah," Ransom interrupted. "I know, it goes against protocol. Do it anyway."

"I'll get started on it as soon as I get this SITREP over to Colonel Lindahl," Alec assured him, swiping the photo from the table and tucking it into the side pocket of his camouflage pants. "I should have something for you this afternoon."

"Thanks. I appreciate it."

"Yeah, well, just remember, if you don't like the message, don't shoot the messenger."

"Answer me a question, Ran, 'cuz I'm genuinely interested." Conor tipped his head as he considered Ransom. With his auburn hair and freckles, he might look like somebody's kid brother, but Ransom knew better. The guy was lethal. He also knew more about computers and how to hack into them than anyone in Delta, and his easygoing nature made him a favorite with the team. "Is there anybody you trust? Or do you feel the need to run background checks on everyone you meet? Including pretty girls in ponytails?"

Ransom turned and picked up the dossier that Alec had put together on Abdul Alkazar, the Afghani tribal leader he'd trusted to provide his team with safe passage through his territories.

The man who had betrayed him.

"If there's one thing I've learned, McCallum, it's never to trust anyone."

HANNAH SAT cross-legged on the floor in the middle of the shop, the toes of one bare foot absently tapping in beat to the sweet, simplistic melody of the music she listened to. It was a New Age keyboard and strings ensemble, and they were fast becoming a favorite. She'd just ordered a dozen copies of their latest release, which she planned to sell in her store, but right now she hoped the soothing strains of music would help to calm her frayed nerves. And more than that, she hoped that immersing herself in activity might help her to stop thinking about *him*.

She'd spent the entire day unpacking, and now she sat surrounded by empty cardboard boxes and heaps of crumpled newspaper. Lined up on the reception counter behind her were a multitude of aromatherapy candles, packets of incense sticks and burners, and tiny vials of fragrant oils that she'd already unpacked. She had just started to delve into the box on the floor beside her. Inside were numerous jewel cases that contained crystal pendants strung on delicate silver chains, and an extensive variety of chakra and therapeutic jewelry. There were more boxes that contained semiprecious stones and crystals, and smooth, tumbled mineral stones.

This is what she would concentrate on today—beautiful things, like the music and jewelry that surrounded her. Not the disturbing man who lived in the apartment above hers.

Definitely not *him*.

Or worse, her own unschooled response to him. She cringed each time she thought of what they'd done together, which was like every other second since she'd pulled free of his arms and run back to her apartment like a scared little rabbit. It had been that, or have sex with Ransom Bennett.

Not that he'd pressured her to have sex with him. Or even indicated he wanted to, aside from having his face buried against the crotch of her shorts. Quite the opposite, in fact. He'd seemed perfectly content with bringing her to orgasm. When she thought about how he'd accomplished that, so quickly and without even taking her clothes off, part of her wanted to die of mortification. But another part of her wanted more.

She wanted to push his clothes from his body and savor every gorgeous, muscular inch of him. She wanted to wrap herself around him, sheathe him within her body and saturate herself in his energy. The sheer strength of her desire had frightened her so much that she'd mumbled some lame excuse about having to get to bed, and she'd fled.

She'd spent most of the night replaying the erotic exchange in her mind, and listing the pros and cons of having sex with Ransom Bennett. As long as the sex was consensual, there should be no problem, right? She wasn't looking for an emotional commitment from the man, just a means to release some of the pent-up sexual frustration she'd been experiencing.

But just thinking about having sex with Ransom made her insides curl. There was a part of her that recognized this wasn't your average guy; he might not be so easily satisfied with a quick, one-night stand. Even worse, she might not be, either.

But she wouldn't think of that now.

Humming lightly to herself, she slid a sleek, black bracelet crafted from polished hematite over her wrist. The magnetic stone was purported to have healing properties, and had been a popular seller at her shop in Boston. Hannah angled the bracelet toward the light that filtered in through the glass windows as she thought of everything—and everyone—she'd left behind.

Did her customers wonder where she'd gone? Had anyone made inquiries to the police about her disappearance? She hoped not. Her friend, Maureen, had promised to hang an Out of Business sign on the door so nobody would worry about her. The rent was paid through the next several months, but she supposed she'd need to contact the landlord at some point and let him know she wouldn't be returning. She was making a new start.

She only hoped her new shop here in Cliftondale did half as well as her previous shop. She really needed it to do well. Because if it didn't, she had nothing else to fall back on, and nobody to turn to. Her parents had made it clear to her that any requests for assistance, financial or otherwise, would not be welcome. At least not while she insisted on using her healing abilities.

Not that she'd ever ask. From the moment she'd decided to pursue a career in holistic health, Hannah had been determined to make it without their help. But she wouldn't think of that, either. Right now, she needed to concentrate on getting her fledgling business ready for opening day.

Careful of the fragile items in the box, she pushed herself to her feet and looked around. She was rapidly running out of room to unpack. Until Ransom built her some shelving units, she had no place to display her New Age wares, but she'd wanted to do an inventory of the boxes to ensure everything had arrived from Boston in one piece.

Bending down, she began stuffing the loose newspapers back into the empty boxes to carry them out to the curb, when she heard raised voices outside. At the same time, a movement on the sidewalk attracted her attention. It was a man, and he was digging through the debris she'd put on the curb earlier. Across the street, a group of four boys heckled him and shouted obscenities.

Puzzled, Hannah walked closer to the window for a better view. The boys looked to be about twelve, and although they were clearly trying to get a reaction from the man, Hannah didn't miss how they kept a safe distance away, almost as if they expected him to come after them. She turned her attention to their victim.

She'd seen plenty of homeless people in Boston, but this guy seemed different. He was slightly built, and there was a furtiveness about him that was a little creepy to watch. He reached into the nearest box and dragged out a sheet of crumpled newspaper, then glanced nervously around him before smoothing it against his thigh. His eyes appeared freakishly huge behind the thick lenses of his glasses. Ignoring the boys' catcalls, he scanned the contents of both sides, then crumpled it up and tossed it aside, before grabbing another sheet.

Hannah guessed he was about her father's age, but he couldn't have been more different than her stern, dignified parent. As he bent over the box to scrounge for another sheet of newspaper, his graying ponytail fell forward, half-obscuring his face. He pushed it back with a quick, impatient gesture, taking the opportunity to look swiftly toward her shop, as if he expected her—or someone else—to sneak up on him. His blue jeans were several sizes too large for him, paired with a shirt that looked like it came straight out of some psychedelic sixties movie.

Just like that, Hannah knew he was the man from the house next door. The man with the binoculars—Mike Howard. She remembered what Ransom had said. *He was harmless.* But when he straightened from the pile of cardboard boxes and sidled over to her trash can, she gasped in indignation. He was actually digging through her household rubbish! Tunnel Rat, indeed. Curiosity turned to outrage in less than an instant, and Hannah found herself on the sidewalk, striding toward the man before she really had a chance to consider her actions.

Across the street, the boys were still shouting at him. "Hey, Howard the Coward, what're you doing? Looking for your supper?" They chortled with laughter, before they spied her striding toward him. "Uh-oh, Howard, here comes a *girl!* Better run, you little coward!"

"Hey!" she called toward the man. "You there! Excuse me, but *what* are you doing?"

Mike Howard snapped upright. His eyes, magnified to cartoonish proportions behind the thick lenses, nearly bugged out of his head when he saw Hannah moving in his direction. He looked around him with something like desperation, as if seeking escape. The boys had momentarily stopped taunting him, no doubt hoping to hear what she would say to him. Mike began edging away from Hannah, moving in the direction of his house.

"You don't come near me," he muttered, and pointed at her with a bony hand that clenched a sheet of crushed newspaper.

Hannah jerked to a stop. "Okay," she agreed, putting her hands up. "It's just that…well, I don't think it's very nice to go poking through a person's trash. I mean, you don't know what's in there. You have to be careful. Besides, it's private property."

"It's *public* property," he said defensively, ignoring her cautions. "Once it goes onto the curb, anyone can have it."

"Oh." Hannah looked at him helplessly. She had no idea if what he said was true or not, but decided that arguing the point with him was probably pointless and possibly dangerous. If there was anything in her trash can worth taking, he was welcome to it. Still, it seemed an invasion of her privacy to have some stranger rooting through her garbage. Not to mention it was just plain disgusting.

The man stared at her for a brief instant, as if waiting for her to challenge him, before he glanced quickly around. Then, as Hannah watched, he skirted past her and made a beeline for the house next door, disappearing through the front door as the boys hurled insults at his retreating back.

Hannah blew out a frustrated breath. Great. Not only was the guy a Peeping Tom, but now she had to worry about him picking through her personal refuse. Walking over to the trash can, she picked up the cover that Mike Howard had thrown onto the ground, and replaced it.

"You shouldn't torment that man," she called to the boys.

"Why not? He's a *freak!*" Without waiting for a response, they walked away, shoving each other along the sidewalk.

As she turned back to the shop, a black Range Rover pulled into the driveway. Her heart skipped a beat as she glimpsed Ransom's face behind the windshield. Would it be rude to run back inside and pretend she hadn't seen him? Even as she hesitated, he climbed out and rounded the hood of the vehicle. He wore a pair of cargo shorts and a white, button-down shirt, rolled up at the sleeves and left untucked. With his cropped black hair, wide shoulders, and long legs, he looked good enough to eat. His dark sunglasses made it impossible to determine if he was looking at her, or what he might be thinking.

"Hey," she said in greeting, feeling awkward and self-conscious. Despite the oppressive heat, she wrapped her arms around her middle. "I see you got some lumber and—" She stopped in mid-sentence and stared at his legs. His bare legs, where she could see muscles flexing from his knees all the way down to his ankles. "You got your cast off!"

"Yeah. I told you it was just a precaution. No big deal." His voice sounded gravelly, like it hurt to talk. Reaching up, he unfastened the long boards he'd strapped to the roof of the vehicle, and angled them over one shoulder. As he turned to walk past her, she saw the grooves etched into the sides of his mouth, and knew his headache had returned. "I guess now you don't have an excuse to come up in the middle of the night to see me."

Hannah's imagination surged. "Oh," she said innocently. "Do I need one?"

He paused, and even with his dark glasses covering his eyes, Hannah felt his gaze sweep over her. "Lady," he said, his voice dropping to the now familiar octave that sent her pulse skittering, "I aim to please. You come on up anytime you feel the need."

Hannah stared at his retreating back for just an instant, as warmth flowed through her. Then she hurried ahead of him to open the door to her shop. "Your headache is back, isn't it? Jeez, you shouldn't be carrying that lumber. Are you sure your foot is okay? Maybe I should just check it."

Ransom eased the lumber through the door and then jerked his sunglasses from his face. He stared at the room with something like horror in his eyes. "*Jesus Christ.* Hannah, I can't work in here like this. Hell, there isn't even enough free space to set up a saw."

"Sorry." Hannah took one look at him, and began stuffing discarded newspapers into the empty boxes. His face was drawn, and his eyes were red-rimmed with fatigue. But it wasn't just his headache drawing his brows together. Clearly, something was eating at him.

"I wasn't expecting you back so soon. I'll have this cleaned up in no time. Then we can go upstairs for a treatment."

If she thought he'd jump at the opportunity, she was wrong. Instead of acknowledging her offer, he leaned the lumber against the wall and bent over to help her. Picking up a piece of crumpled newsprint, he smoothed it out and read the top. He pressed his fingers into his eyes as if trying to focus, and frowned. "The *Boston Gazette,* dated a month ago," he mused. He slid her a meaningful glance and snapped the paper open to a better position. "Well, now, let's just see what was going on in *Boston* last month, shall we?"

His voice dripped with sarcasm, as if he'd known full well she'd been full of crap when she said she hadn't been in Massachusetts recently.

Hannah snatched the sheet from him and crumpled it up into a ball. "Why don't I get you something cold to drink, instead? I can see your head hurts, and it's no wonder. It's so hot outside, and you must be thirsty after carrying that lumber."

God, she was babbling like an idiot. Maybe it was the expression of disappointment on his face, as if he knew all her secrets and had fully expected her to share them with him. And in not doing so, she'd somehow let him down.

Before he could answer, there was a knock at the door to the shop. Hannah couldn't help herself; she started violently and clutched the newspaper against her stomach. Ransom frowned, but whether it was directed at her or the unwelcome intrusion, she couldn't tell.

He arched an eyebrow. "You're going to have to get used to people coming in here," he commented drily, and stepped forward to open the door.

A man stood outside on the step, looking at the banner in the shop window. Peering around Ransom's shoulder, Hannah could see he was young, probably in his early twenties. He wore a pair of chinos and a lime-green polo shirt. With his tousled, sandy hair and smooth features, he was the epitome of the all-American boy-next-door. He carried a small notepad and pen in one hand, and a digital camera in the other.

"Sorry, pal," Ransom growled, "whatever you're selling, we're not buying."

"Are you the owner of this shop?" he asked, craning his neck around Ransom to peer inside.

"I'm the owner." Hannah stepped forward. She didn't miss how Ransom kept his body between her and the visitor. "Is there a problem?"

The man's eyebrows flew up in surprise. "No, ma'am," he said with a quick smile. "My name is Bob Carroll and I work for the Cliftondale News." He gestured toward the windows that overlooked the street. "I saw your grand-opening banner, and was hoping I could do a story. For the paper." When Hannah didn't answer, he smiled encouragingly. "It's free advertising. We have a circulation of over twenty-five thousand, not to mention our online readership."

Hannah felt her chest constrict. He wanted to do a story. About her. About her shop. A story that would be accessible online to anyone with a computer. All it would take for Sully to find her would be a Google search, and the story would pop up.

"Thanks anyway," she said briskly, and stepped around Ransom to put her hand on the door handle, "but I'm going to have to refuse."

Poor Bob actually looked taken aback. With his collegiate

good looks and easygoing manner, he probably wasn't familiar with the word *no,* at least coming from the opposite sex. "Well, at least let me get some basic information from you," he persisted. "What do you sell in your shop?"

"Reiki," she said shortly. "Just Reiki."

She tried to close the door, but to her horror, he forestalled her by putting his foot against the bottom. Unless she really threw her weight against it, she had no choice but to let him finish talking. Ransom didn't try to intervene. Hannah was acutely conscious of him looking at her with an expression of quiet speculation.

"Well, that sounds interesting," Bob said, jotting it down on his pad of paper. "But an interview would enable me to put a nice, personal spin on it." He gave her an engaging smile. "Are you sure you won't reconsider? The article would run two days before the grand opening. People as far away as Fayetteville read this paper. It might bring more customers in."

"Thank you," Hannah repeated in a firm voice, "but the answer is still no."

Bob's expression was one of bewilderment. "You're kidding, right?"

"Sorry, Bob, I'm not." She felt panicky. She wanted him gone. She wanted him to forget he ever had a thought about writing an article about her business.

"Well, then, at least let me take a picture of the outside of the shop," he said. "You don't have to do an interview, but I can run a small blurb with an accompanying photo on the back page."

Hannah smiled tightly. Realistically, she knew a small paragraph about the shop would probably fly under the radar and never even make it onto the Internet. If he was satisfied with taking a photo and writing a blurb, then so was she. She just wanted him gone. "Fine. Whatever. Thank you, and goodbye."

She actually had to give Ransom a slight shove in order to

move him out of the way as she closed the door. Even then, Bob didn't leave, and it was all Hannah could do not to wrench the door open again and shoo him off. To her relief, he finally gave a slight shake of his head and turned back toward the sidewalk, where a green sedan was parked at the curb.

Hannah scrubbed her hands over her face. She couldn't believe what she'd just done. Her treatment of the reporter had been incredibly rude, and she hated being rude. Her hands were trembling, and she determinedly shoved them into the pockets of her shorts.

"Well, that was interesting," drawled Ransom. She turned to see him leaning against the wall with his arms crossed over his chest, watching her. She knew his head was throbbing; it was there in his tense expression and in the way he moved, deliberately and very carefully, as if any quick motions caused him pain. "Care to explain why you turned the kid away?"

"No," she said curtly, "I don't."

How could she explain it to him? What would she say? Her fear that a newspaper article might lead Sully to her doorstep wasn't the only reason she'd refused the interview. She knew firsthand how the media could twist the truth into something sordid and salacious. But there was no way she could tell Ransom how she'd once been raked through the muck by journalists who looked every bit as sweet and harmless as Bob Carroll. By the time the Boston papers had finished with her, she'd had no choice but to close her shop. How could he understand what she'd been through? Even her own family hadn't understood.

She risked a glance at Ransom. He had his eyes closed. He pinched the bridge of his nose and then opened his eyes to look at her. His expression said clearly that while he might be in pain, there was no way he'd let her bullshit him.

"Look," she finally said, "I'd just rather not talk to a reporter, okay? Some people don't get it, and I wouldn't want him to misunderstand what it is that I do." She paused. "Like you did."

Ransom's lips lifted in a half smile. "Then doesn't it make sense to explain it to him, instead of letting him talk to the neighbors?"

What? Hannah followed Ransom's gaze through the window, and gasped. Howard the Coward had returned. He stood on the sidewalk talking with Bob the reporter. As Hannah watched, Mike Howard opened a sheet of newspaper and showed it to the reporter, even as he pointed directly toward the shop.

Hannah closed her eyes briefly. *Damn, damn, damn.* She could only guess what incriminating words were printed on that sheath of newsprint, or what Bob the reporter might make of them. Opening her eyes, she watched as the two men spoke briefly, then Bob actually shook Mike Howard's hand before climbing into his car and driving away.

Don't be angry. Don't be worried. Be grateful.

Hannah repeated the words silently. They were three of the five principles of Reiki, and had gotten her through more difficult days than she cared to remember. She realized now that it had been a huge mistake not to talk to the reporter. In being rude to him, she'd opened herself up for negative Karma. But it wasn't too late; she could still call the newspaper and agree to talk to him.

Drawing in a deep breath, she turned back to Ransom, who stood watching her with an inscrutable expression in his dark eyes.

"Something going on that you'd like to share with me?" His voice was flat, as if he already knew the answer.

"Actually, yes," she said.

She'd surprised him, she could tell. He'd thought she was going to give him the brush-off, assure him that everything was fine. But in this instance, she'd made a quick decision to tell Ransom about Mike Howard. "I think the man next door is stalking me."

Ransom's eyebrows drew together. "Mike Howard? I told you—"

"I know what you said," Hannah interrupted, stepping closer to him. She caught his scent, an alluring mixture of sandalwood and soap. "But I found him going through my trash this morning, and he seems overly interested in what I'm doing. He watches me. *With binoculars*. And now he's talking to that reporter about me. I'm telling you, there's something really creepy about him."

Ransom swore softly. "Okay, I'll take care of it."

Hannah shivered. "How? How are you going to take care of it, Ransom? What are you going to do, threaten the man? Or beat him up? Jeez, you sound like—" She stopped abruptly, aware of what she'd been about to say. *You sound like Sully.* He would have no compunctions about taking care of a problem through the use of threats or physical violence.

His eyes flashed with what might have been anger, and then it was gone. "That wouldn't be very neighborly, now would it? Look, Howard's paranoid, but he's not dangerous. I'll talk with him. Again. Okay?"

"Okay. Great." Hannah wrapped her arms around herself, but couldn't prevent her gaze from sliding to the windows that faced Mike Howard's house. She didn't really believe Ransom could do anything to prevent Mike Howard from spying on her, but at least she'd distracted him from asking her any awkward questions about Boston. "I can see your headache is bothering you. Do you want me to give you a treatment?"

"Yeah," he said softly. "Actually, I do."

Something flared in his eyes and caused Hannah's stomach to tighten in anticipation. He advanced toward her, and she took an involuntary step back. What was he doing? His mood was dark and unpredictable, and something inside Hannah responded to it, made her want to abandon herself to him and see just how far he'd be willing to go.

"Okay," she said, aware her voice sounded breathless. "If you're ready, then so am I."

He took another step toward her, and without thinking about what she was doing, Hannah reached up to touch him.

9

RANSOM'S BREATH hissed in when she laid a hand against his chest. For a moment, he thought his head would explode. Then it passed, and there was just Hannah, barely reaching his shoulder, with her warm fingers still pressed against his skin. He wondered if she could feel the heavy beating of his heart beneath her palm.

The pounding behind his eyes receded, but now he was way too aware of everything else. Like how good she smelled, and how tempting she looked in her flowered sundress, held in place over her shoulders by two ridiculous little bow ties.

If he tugged on them, would the bodice of her dress slip all the way down to her waist, or would it catch on the small, erect peaks of her breasts?

He'd told himself that no matter how much he wanted to, he wouldn't sleep with Hannah. Not when he could go wheels up in a matter of days. Not when he couldn't even explain to her where he was going, or how long he might be gone.

Not when he couldn't say with any certainty that he'd even come back alive.

But when she stood there, staring up at him with big, blue eyes that silently begged him to touch her, he knew he couldn't resist.

Not a chance.

Not when he couldn't even keep his hands from reaching for her.

"Wait." Hannah glanced meaningfully toward the side window that faced Mike Howard's house. "Why don't we go to my apartment? I can get you something to drink, and take care of you properly."

Christ. Her words, combined with the sensual expression on her face, caused his body to respond. His imagination surged. He didn't know if she was referring to his nearly forgotten headache, or the raging hard-on he'd developed when she'd touched him, but he found he didn't really care.

He just wanted her to touch him.

He *needed* her to touch him. In a way that had nothing to do with healing, and everything to do with the lust ricocheting through his gut.

Right now, he didn't even care that Doc Katz had recommended he take leave until he was completely recovered. He'd refused, but he knew the doctor's recommendation was probably sitting on his commanding officer's desk. Ransom was pretty much just waiting to be yanked off the mission.

But at this moment, all he could think about was Hannah. He shouldn't want her. She wasn't his type, but he was having a hell of a time convincing his body of that.

"Yeah," he finally managed, proving that his brain cells had definitely migrated south. His voice sounded rough and completely unlike himself. "Let's lock up here."

Hannah swallowed hard but handed him the key to the shop. She waited on the sidewalk while he secured the door and then preceded him into the cool, shadowed interior of the hallway. He loved watching her walk. He could see the individual bumps of her spine above the top edge of her dress and, holy shit…was that a tattoo just beneath her shoulder blade?

When she bent to unlock her apartment door, he inspected it more closely. Yep. Definitely a tiny dragonfly tattoo.

He followed her into her apartment, pausing just long enough to lock the door behind them. Instead of leading him through the living room toward the small spare room where her Reiki table was set up, she turned to face him.

Her cheeks were flushed, and her blue eyes—her incredibly blue eyes—seemed to shimmer as she looked at him. He waited, when every cell in his body wanted to haul her against him and devour her.

"There's something I need to say to you before..." Her voice trailed off and she colored prettily. Taking a deep breath, she continued. "I—I was thinking about you this morning. About us." The words tumbled out fast, like she was afraid if she didn't spill them right away, she might not get them out at all. She twirled the silver ring on her right hand. "About what happened last night...in the back room of the shop."

Oh, yeah. Like he hadn't thought about the same thing at least a hundred times. He didn't tell her that, given the chance, he'd do it again in a heartbeat, only this time there would be no clothing to hinder him.

She chewed her lip, and he saw the uncertainty in her expression.

Shit. This was where she'd tell him that she couldn't sleep with him unless there was a commitment of some kind. That she couldn't give herself to a man—any man—without some kind of emotional bonding. Although, come to think of it, they hadn't actually talked about having sex. Shit. Had he been wrong? Had he read her wrong? Was this all about giving him a Reiki treatment, and nothing more?

"I'm listening."

Her breathing had quickened, but she tipped her chin up and determinedly met his eyes. "I know you said I'm not your type, and maybe that's true. But there's no denying there's a—a chemistry between us. Don't you agree?"

More like nitroglycerin—unstable and highly sensitive. Liable to explode without warning. "There's something there," he agreed.

She read the meaning in his voice and her face turned rosier. Ransom watched in fascination as the glow spread down her neck and disappeared beneath the edge of her sundress. Just how far did that blush extend? He fully intended to find out, and took a step forward, only to be halted by her hand on his chest.

Sensation vibrated through him.

Hannah stared up at him. "I just want you to know that I'm not looking for a commitment. It's actually the last thing I want. I just think that…well, sometimes sex can be a powerful restorative. Just the act of touching another person can release endorphins that actually speed the healing process."

Whatever Ransom had expected her to say, that wasn't it. Was she actually trying to promote sex with him as part of her freaking treatment? She made it sound like she was doing him a favor. Like sleeping with him wouldn't mean a thing to her beyond an act of philanthropy.

Not that he believed her. He knew how to read people and he'd pegged her for a good girl the moment he'd met her. The kind of girl you brought home to meet your parents.

The kind of girl you married.

But then again, what did he know? After all, he'd been wrong about Alkazar.

"Good," he said gruffly. "That sounds great, because I can't make any promises to you, either." He looked down at her hand on his chest. "We'll think of this as alternative medicine, okay? Maybe it'll be something for the medical journals. Think of it— every soldier in the armed services will hope to get his bell rung, just so he can qualify for the treatment."

She couldn't quite suppress a smile at his outrageous suggestion. But when she looked at him, her eyes were serious. "So long as you understand that the only soldier I want to treat is *you.*"

As much as he wanted to scoop Hannah into his arms and stride with her to the nearest bed, he moved slowly, covering her hand with his and entwining their fingers so that he could pull her toward him. It was still broad daylight, and he could read each thought, each emotion, as it passed across her face. She wanted him, but she was as nervous as a green recruit. He drew her closer still, until their bodies almost touched.

Her breathing hitched as he moved his hands up the length of her bare arms and over her shoulders. He paused at the ribbons there. She stopped breathing. Reaching behind her, he pulled her hair free from the ponytail holder, watching as it tumbled in thick, sleek waves around her cheeks. He threaded his fingers through the cool, honeyed length, enjoying how it slipped through his hands. The afternoon sunlight caught the highlights and turned them to pure gold.

Ransom squinted toward the window as a shaft of pain knifed behind his eyes. "Christ, I thought after yesterday, you'd have put some damned shades up."

Despite his visit with Howard, there was no guarantee the guy wouldn't decide to check out the early show.

"Sorry." Her voice was husky and a little breathless. "Come with me." Reaching up, she caught his hand and led him down the short corridor to—*whoa*—not the Reiki room, but her bedroom.

It was a lot like her, soft and refreshing. Wooden plantation blinds were closed across the windows, casting the room in soft, afternoon shadows. A ceiling fan turned lazily overhead. White beadboard covered the walls and an ancient, iron-framed bed, heaped with pillows, dominated the small room.

Clusters of white candles stood on the dresser and jewelry spilled out of two different boxes. Small, colored vials of perfumes and creams and cosmetics were arranged neatly on a mirrored tray, next to what looked like an assortment of colored rocks. The room even smelled good, like clean linen and citrus. Everything was tidily in its place, and only the boxes pushed against the wall disturbed the calm tranquility of the space.

Hannah released his hand and stood uncertainly for a moment, as if seeking reassurance. "I hope this is okay…."

Was she kidding? "It's great."

She clasped her hands together and looked around the room, as if seeing it through his eyes. "I just moved a bunch of stuff into the spare room, so the atmosphere in there isn't quite as restful as this room."

"Of course." She was totally bullshitting him.

"So…if you'll lie down on the bed, I'll do a treatment for you." Her voice was overly bright, as if to mask her uncertainty.

Without answering, Ransom sat down on the edge of the bed and bent to remove his sandals, keeping his eyes on Hannah. She drew a long, wooden match from a slender box inside her dresser drawer. As he watched, she touched the flame to each of the candles, until the top of the dresser was awash with flickering light. Her glaze darted toward him. "Lighting the candles helps clear any negative energy from the room."

"Wow." He tried to sound interested, but all he really wanted was her, naked in his arms. "What are the rocks for?"

"These?" Hannah picked up one of the multifaceted stones. It was small and unevenly shaped, tinged with dark yellow. "These are crystals. This one is a citrine crystal, for creativity." She closed her fingers around it. "If you hold it in your palm, you can feel the energy that flows through it."

He had something she could hold in her palm, with plenty of energy flowing through it, but he kept that thought to himself.

"Each crystal has its own unique properties that make it bene-ficial," she continued. "There's even a crystal that will keep your computer working—"

"Hannah."

She stopped mid-sentence, looking sheepish. "I'm sorry. I'm just not very good at this."

"I'm not keeping score," he said softly. "Just do what you *are* good at. Come put your hands on me, and don't think about the rest."

AS HANNAH WATCHED, Ransom lay on his back on her bed—holy cow, on *her* bed—and stretched his long, bare legs out on the covers, bending his arms behind his head and reminding her of the night she'd first met him, when he'd looked like a decadent offering from the gods.

She was as nervous as a high-school freshman on her first date, which was just ridiculous. She'd had relationships before, even one or two that had been based more on sex than any emotional connection. While she wasn't an advocate of one-night stands, she recognized that sometimes your body craved the close, physical contact that only sex could bring.

But just the thought of having sex with Ransom Bennett was enough to give her a serious case of the jitters. There was no doubt in her mind that he was way above her pay grade. Guys like him hooked up with gorgeous, tough-as-nails women with plenty of attitude. Women who looked like they would just as soon kill a man as kiss him. Not women like herself, who believed in energy healing and flower therapy, and who tucked tail and ran at the first sign of adversity.

For half a second, she stood undecided. Every cell in her body ached to touch him, but she hesitated. There was a stillness about him that had nothing to do with tranquility or quiet. It was like watching a big cat in the seconds before it pounced, when every muscle was tightly coiled and each sense focused intently on its prey.

His gaze slid over her, taking in every detail of her appearance, lingering on her face before dropping lower to her breasts, and then down to her bare legs beneath the hem of the sundress.

His expression was hungry, and it gave Hannah the courage to step toward him.

The mattress sagged as she climbed onto the bed. Scooting closer to Ransom, she sat cross-legged so that she had only to lean forward to reach every part of him. She hadn't even touched him, yet her hands heated in anticipation. She risked a glance at his face and saw he watched her through hooded eyes. Her blood began a slow, hot glide against the underside of her skin.

"So tell me more about this thing you do," he murmured, his eyes never leaving hers. "This...Reiki."

Hannah allowed him the smallest of smiles, but loaded it with meaning. "I'd rather show you, instead."

She leaned over him and pushed her fingers through the rough silk of his hair, laying her palms flat against the top of his head. His breath hissed in, and for just an instant, pain pricked behind her eyes and then vanished, leaving her acutely conscious of the man beneath her.

He'd closed his eyes and his breathing was shallow. Even if she hadn't felt his pain for herself, the furrow between his eyebrows and the lines alongside his mouth gave him away. Hannah concentrated on opening herself up to the energy of Reiki, but found herself completely distracted by his scent. Shampoo and sandalwood, and clean, male sweat. The combination was intoxicating.

His muscles were tense, a sure sign of discomfort. Guiltily, Hannah pushed aside her awareness of him as a man, at least until his pain abated. When had channeling energy become so difficult? She found she couldn't think clearly when he was this close. She wanted to slide her palms down the sides of his face, cup his lean cheeks in her hands and kiss him until they were both breathless.

"You're doing fine," she said, but whether she spoke the words to herself or to Ransom, she wasn't sure. Her voice sounded husky, and she strove for a more affirmative tone. "I can already sense the pain isn't as severe as it was that first night."

He made a grunting sound of agreement.

"This is the Crown Chakra. This position helps establish a sense of balance throughout the body. Do you feel that?" The palms of her hands began to grow warm and tingly. "Do you feel any heat?"

"Oh, yeah," he breathed.

Something in his tone made her glance down. With a sense of mild shock, she realized his eyes were open, and he had a perfect view down the front of her dress to her bare breasts. Instead of embarrassment, Hannah felt a thrill of naughty excitement course through her.

"You know," she said, biting her lip and giving him a guileless look, "I can't really achieve the right angle from where I'm sitting." She rose on her knees over him and braced both hands on his shoulders. "Would it be okay if I, um, straddled your hips?"

Something flared, hot and fierce, in his eyes before he quickly banked it. "Be my guest," he offered. "Never let it be said that I didn't accommodate a lady's request to achieve the perfect... angle."

He didn't touch her, but Hannah knew he missed nothing as she adjusted her skirt and gingerly positioned herself over him, so that her bare thighs bracketed his lean body. Her pulse quickened when she lowered herself onto him and realized her silken panties were no barrier against the hard, thick length of him beneath his cargo shorts. His obvious arousal caused an answering tremor of excitement to shiver through her, and it was all she could do not to press herself more fully against him.

She slid one hand beneath his head to cup the nape of his neck, while placing her free hand at the base of his throat. His skin was hot, and his pulse beat strongly against her fingertips. The position required her to lean slightly forward in order to reach him, and the movement pushed her flush against his erection. Immediately, her body grew wet with desire, and it took all of Hannah's self-control not to rub sensuously back and forth along his length.

"This is called the Throat Chakra. This position helps high blood pressure," she said breathlessly, unable to meet his eyes. "It's also good for self-expression."

"Look at me." It wasn't a request. It was a command, delivered in a rough, husky voice that Hannah was helpless to resist. Slowly, she dragged her focus upward from where her hands encircled the strong column of his neck, and a needy shudder worked through her as she met the smoldering heat in his eyes. "Whatever it is you're doing…" he rasped, "don't stop."

His words caused her pulse to kick into overdrive. "Reiki," she whispered, knowing she lied. "I'm doing Reiki. And I have no intention of stopping."

She stared at him in the muted light, admiring the play of shadows across his chiseled features. He had a beautiful mouth. More than anything, she wanted to rub her thumb over the fullness of his lower lip, and then test the sensitive inner flesh with her tongue. She knew firsthand the wicked, delicious things Ransom was capable of doing with his mouth and suddenly, she was eager to experience those sensations again. And this time, she wouldn't let him stop her.

She maintained the Reiki position. Heat still flowed through her palms where they rested against his skin, but she was no longer consciously aware of transmitting energy.

She was only aware of Ransom.

Her pulse was a languorous thudding through her veins, and she could almost imagine it matched the throb of his heartbeat beneath her fingers.

Concentrate.

Removing her hands from his neck, she slid them down to the

top button of his shirt, glancing at his face to see his reaction to this new exploration. He arched an eyebrow at her but said nothing. Emboldened, she slipped the top button free, then the next, spreading the material as she moved downward.

Within the vee of fabric, his exposed flesh was smooth and brown. Hannah's finger itched to stroke him. She was aware that her breathing had quickened. She undid a third button, then a fourth, revealing the shallow indentation beneath his breastbone, and the ridges of muscle that fingered their way down his rib cage.

"Oh…" She breathed a sigh of admiration as she unfastened the last button and separated the edges of his shirt. She'd seen him bare-chested before, but the lighting had been bad and she hadn't had a true appreciation for just how big and hard he was *everywhere.*

Now she watched, entranced, as a waft of cool air across his skin caused his nipples to harden into small buds, and raised tiny goose bumps across his chest. When she impulsively stroked her fingers across the sensitized flesh, his muscles contracted and his stomach tightened. Beneath the fabric of his cargo shorts, his arousal pushed against her and she shifted restlessly, seeking more of the delicious contact.

Hannah didn't know what she found more erotic—the physical reaction of his body to her touch, or the heat in his eyes. Just the knowledge that he watched her caused her own nipples to contract into tight, aching peaks.

Taking her time, she smoothed her palms over the rise of his pectorals, reveling in their strength. As if drawn by some unseen force, her fingers once more sought his nipples with her fingertips, brushing ever so lightly across their pebbled tips and drawing a small hiss of pleasure from him.

With one hand covering the small space between his collarbones, Hannah positioned her other hand in the shallow groove between his pectorals, feeling the hard thump of his heart beneath her palm.

"Right now, I'm focusing on the Heart Chakra," she said, locking her gaze with his. "This position increases the flow of love and compassion."

"It must be working," he said, his voice no more than a low growl, "because I love whatever it is you're doing." He uncurled his arms from where they were still bent behind his head, and moved them to her waist. "In fact, I can't remember the last time I felt this good."

He felt pretty good to her, too.

Hannah swallowed hard. His hands at her waist were big and warm, and when he slid them to her hips, it was all she could do not to mimic his movements and smooth her hands over his body in return. She was unprepared, however, when he stroked his palms down the length of her thighs and then back up again, capturing her skirt in his fingers and pushing it to her waist.

"Ransom."

"Shh," he soothed her. "You just keep on doing what you're doing. I'm going to practice a little energy transmission of my own."

"It—it doesn't work like that," she gasped, as his hands moved up under her dress. "You're not trained in Reiki."

"Maybe not," he agreed, his voice hoarse, "but I guess I know a thing or two about channeling energy."

His words caused her insides to vibrate with anticipation as all thoughts of continuing Reiki vanished. She bit her lip as his hands smoothed beneath the skirt of her sundress and cupped her rear, his fingers splaying over her buttocks and applying subtle downward pressure until her softness molded itself over the hard ridge of his arousal.

"Oh," she breathed, and unable to help herself, she rocked against him. The sensation was an exquisite torture as intense pleasure spiraled through her. She wanted more but couldn't get close enough. He had too many clothes on.

"That's it," he rasped, and with his hands gripping and kneading the softness of her bottom, he thrust his hips upward. His face was taut, the expression in his eyes so intent that it stole Hannah's breath. "Tell me what you feel," he demanded softly.

Like I'm going to die if you don't touch me.

HER GUTTURAL MOAN, combined with the rocking of her hips against him, nearly undid Ransom. Hannah's eyelashes had drifted closed, and a tiny frown furrowed the smoothness between her eyebrows as she nibbled on her lower lip. The sight of her concentrating so fully on achieving pleasure mesmerized him.

One strap of her sundress slipped down over her shoulder, dragging the top of her bodice with it and revealing a creamy hint of breast. Ransom sucked in a breath.

Go. Slow.

He wanted to devour her. Since that night in the shop, he'd thought of little else but Hannah Hartwell. Of possessing her, of driving her as crazy as she was driving him. But this time, he wouldn't stop until they were both satisfied.

Her hands had slid down his torso and he didn't think she was even aware of how her fingers had curled around the waistband of his shorts, clutching him as if she was some kind of dainty cowgirl riding a bronco.

With his hands still squeezing her bottom, he encouraged her to move over him, gritting his teeth against the pleasure, entranced by the rapt expression on her face.

"Oh," she sighed, "this wasn't… This feels too good."

Her face was a portrait of sublime pleasure, and Ransom felt hot lust pool behind the zipper of his shorts. Freeing his hands from beneath her dress, he cupped the nape of her neck and drew her down until he could slant his mouth across hers, absorbing her small gasp of surprise. For just an instant, she remained rigid and unresponsive.

Then she was kissing him.

Holy God, he didn't think he'd ever been kissed so thoroughly before. It was like someone had opened a floodgate of sexual need. Hot, deep kisses that sent lust jackknifing through him and caused his shorts to feel about two sizes too small.

She still rocked back against him, but now her hands were on his body, touching him everywhere, skimming over his rib cage and tracing along the ridges of his muscles. She smoothed her palms along the undersides of his arms, pushing them over his head and skating her fingers along their length until they tangled with his, locking together. Her tongue was making slippery passes at his, alternately licking and sucking, as she mewled softly with need and pleasure.

Christ. He needed to regain some control, needed to slow things down before they got completely out of control.

Hannah pulled her mouth from his. He lay there, dragging air into his lungs and feeling as if he'd just done a forty-mile ruck-trek. His limbs were weak, and his head felt light. He forced himself to focus on Hannah, but he only had a glimpse of her eyes, hazy with desire, and her lips, lush and wet from kissing him, before she skated her mouth along the line of his jaw and caught his earlobe between her small, perfect teeth.

He groaned when she swirled her tongue against his ear, and then his heart nearly stopped when she pulled one hand free and, reaching between their bodies, cupped him through the heavy material of his shorts. She didn't do more than just lay her hand over him, but it was enough for him to stop breathing.

"Mmm," she whispered in a husky voice. "You smell delicious, and you taste good enough to eat. In fact—" she paused to plant a moist kiss against his neck "—I may do just that."

Before he could protest—*as if*—she shimmied back on his

thighs and slowly kissed her way down the length of his torso, lingering for several long, erotic seconds over his nipples to lave each with slow, lazy laps of her tongue.

Ransom groaned. The fingers of his free hand were still entwined with hers, and now he released them to bury both hands in the silken softness of her hair, reveling in the feel of it as it drifted across his stomach during her downward journey.

"Hannah. Jesus."

She'd reached the edge of his waistband, and was gently scraping her teeth across the taut muscles of his abdomen and making low noises of approval as her fingers worked the button of his shorts. Glancing down, he found the sight of her honey-blond hair spread across his stomach, and her bare shoulders rising over his groin extremely erotic. It was like his wildest, teenage fantasy come true, and suddenly he felt as inexperienced and awkward as a sixteen-year-old virgin.

Hell, when had sex become so unpredictable? Granted, it had been a while since he'd done the nasty, but in his experience, sex involved a reliable and proven series of steps, not unlike a military mission. Women wanted to talk, and then touch. Touching led to kissing, which segued into heavy petting which, if he played his cards right, led to sex.

And where sex was concerned, he was accustomed to being the action guy, the one who *did* versus the one being done. Maybe it was his choice of women. There was no question that the area surrounding Camp Lejeune and Fort Bragg boasted its fair share of military groupies—women who were only interested in soldiers who sported Special Operations patches on their shoulders. Not that any of the women he'd ever been with had any idea that he was Delta Force. As far as they were concerned, he was just a regular infantry guy who knew what to do with his hands.

In his relationships—if you could call them that—the

women begged and he accommodated them. But he never lost his self-control. No matter how hot the woman was, or how sweetly she cried out for him to just *do her,* he maintained a certain amount of self-discipline. Even his orgasms were controlled to coincide with his partner's. He never, ever came first. Yep, he was a real gentleman.

But now, with Hannah nibbling and licking at his stomach, and her fingers plucking at the fastening of his shorts, he wondered how long he might last. Christ, she hadn't even *touched* him, and he was close to exploding.

Reaching down, he caught her face in between his palms and drew her up. Her eyes were bright with desire, her lips lush and pink from kissing him, and when she smiled questioningly at him, he knew he was a goner.

"Let me," she pleaded softly, and bent quickly to examine the button on his shorts, fumbling briefly with it. "God, I want to see you…"

Ransom heard the zipper rasp downward an instant before cool air wafted over his exposed flesh. He closed his eyes on Hannah's soft exclamation, as she freed him from his briefs. His breath rushed out of his lungs in a rough whoosh when she ran her fingertips over the biggest, hardest erection he'd ever had.

"Wow," she murmured, "and to think, I never even got to the Root Chakra."

What?

Then she closed her hand around him, and his head fell back against the pillows with a heartfelt groan of pleasure.

"Why do you think they call it the Root Chakra, anyway?" she asked, and he could hear the smile in her voice. "But I think you have way too many clothes on. Can't we do something about these?"

Ransom was breathing hard. He looked at her, kneeling over him, her breasts nearly spilling out of her sundress, holding his straining cock in her hand and suddenly he was done waiting.

"You first," he growled.

Reaching down, he fisted his hands in the fabric of her sundress and pulled the entire garment over her head, ignoring her gasp of surprise. When he would have pulled it completely free, she snatched the material and clutched it against herself, staring at him with something like panic in her eyes.

"I want to see you," he said, his voice no more than a rough rasp.

Slowly, he tugged the material from her hands until she had no choice but to release it. Ransom felt something shift in his chest at the expression of stark vulnerability on her face.

"Hannah," he said softly. "I want to see you...all of you."

Wild color bloomed in her cheeks, and she chewed her lower lip. "I'm going to disappoint you. You said you liked women with more T & A than I'm sporting..."

But she didn't resist when he caught her hands in his and slowly drew them out wide, until there was nothing of her he couldn't see.

He swallowed hard.

Hannah Hartwell was small, there was no denying it. But everything about her was perfectly formed, from the high, sweet mounds of her breasts with their rosy nipples, to the inward sweep of her waist and her flat tummy, to the gentle flare of her hips where she straddled him, and where his impatient cock was now pressed up against her.

"Babe," he croaked, "I'm not disappointed. I'm completely and utterly blown away by how fucking gorgeous you are."

He hadn't meant to be quite so crude, but was rewarded when she smiled shyly and pulled one hand free from his to reach down and stroke a finger across the blunt head of his erection.

"Ditto."

"Take these off," he said roughly, and pushed his hands into the waistband of her panties, shoving them down over her hips, gratified when she helped by kicking them free until she was completely naked.

When she straddled him again, Ransom almost wept with sheer joy. Except for a narrow strip of dark blond hair riding above her cleft, she was completely smooth and pink, and Ransom felt himself swell even more at the sight of her feminine folds.

"Goddamn. You're so...*bare.*"

Ransom watched as she flushed beneath his regard. "I had a Brazilian wax," she admitted shyly. "It was my first. Is it okay?"

A rough burst of delighted laughter escaped him. "Sweetheart, it's more than okay—it's incredible."

He wanted nothing more than to turn her beneath him and bury himself deep inside her body. But, damn, she was so small, he was actually a little afraid. He hadn't lied when he said he preferred bigger women, since he didn't have to worry overly much about being too rough. Women like Hannah, however, were a different story altogether. She was delicate. He suspected that no matter how aroused she was, their joining might not be easy. Normally, that would be enough to have him hightailing it in the opposite direction.

But not this time.

He found himself transfixed by the sight of her.

"Ah, babe," he groaned, "I have to touch you."

Without waiting for her response, he cupped her breasts in his hands. If asked, he'd have said he preferred big-breasted women, but the sight of his large hands completely covering her gave him a strange sense of satisfaction. He gently squeezed her breasts, testing their weight, before rolling his fingers over her nipples. Hannah made a sound of pleasure and covered his hands with her own, encouraging him to continue. Kneading one breast, he reached down with his other hand and palmed her. She was like hot silk against his skin. She pushed herself against his fingers, and he felt her wetness, and knew she was more than ready for him.

"Omigod," she gasped, "I have to… I have to…"

Ransom was unprepared when she rose up and, still gripping his cock in her hand, guided him into position. When she rubbed the sensitive head of his erection along her slick cleft, teasing her clitoris, he had to clench his teeth to retain control.

But when she would have pushed herself down over him, he grabbed her hips with both hands, preventing her from bringing him into her body.

"Hannah. *Wait.* Christ, we don't even have a condom."

"I'm on the pill," she gasped, her fingers holding him, stroking him, pushing him to the brink, "and I promise you I'm clean."

"Yeah, I believe you," he croaked, desperate to slow her down, "but we still need protection, babe. Just give me a sec…"

She was still rotating her hips over him, and Ransom knew that if she wasn't telling the truth—if she really *wasn't* on the pill—just sliding along her wet folds could be enough to impregnate her. But his wallet was in his back pocket, and as he shifted his hips to reach beneath himself, he lost his grip on Hannah as she rubbed herself sensuously along his erection.

Free of his restraining hold, she suddenly raised herself over him, and before he could object or jerk away, she slid down onto him in one firm movement, sheathing him fully within her tight heat. Ransom gave a hoarse cry, but whether in protest or pleasure, he didn't know.

The sensation of being buried inside her was so incredibly good that he let her move over him for several long, reckless strokes. Pleasure built until his sac contracted, and he knew his self-control was tenuous. A part of him was tempted to let her continue, but he still retained a tiny grasp on his sanity, and swiftly lifted her off him, setting her back on his thighs.

The expression of need on her face nearly undid him, and with shaking fingers, he found the condom and tore it free, sheathing himself quickly.

"We have to use these, babe," he said, lifting her again and positioning her over his hard flesh. "You don't want to play those kinds of games, trust me."

Trust me.

Yeah, right.

She wouldn't even tell him what city she was from.

And then it no longer mattered as she eased herself back down on top of him, her soft gasps of pleasure drowning out the thoughts that raced through his head.

Hannah's face was taut with desire. She caught her lower lip between her teeth and closed her eyes as her body adjusted to his size. He was large, in all respects, and he knew it couldn't be all pleasure that Hannah was feeling. But as he watched, her lips rounded in a perfect *O* of wonder, and she shifted experimentally.

A ragged groan was dragged out of Ransom's throat at the incredible sensation of her inner muscles clamping over him. He couldn't stop his hands from moving to cup her buttocks and guide her up, and then back down over his shaft.

"Oh, oh…I'm going to come," Hannah panted, her face tight with intense pleasure.

Her words, combined with her thighs clenching his hips and the feel of her body fisting around him, were too much. With a rough cry, Ransom gave one powerful thrust upward, surging into her welcoming body and climaxing in long, hot spurts deep inside her.

Hannah shuddered over him and then collapsed forward, her face buried against his neck. The only sound was their breathing, fast and hard. Ransom's hands still covered her bottom, and as he dragged air into his lungs and his vision slowly came back into focus, the enormity of his folly hit him.

He'd just had unprotected sex with a woman he barely knew.

Granted, he'd managed to get a condom on before he'd climaxed, but it could turn out to be a case of too little, too late.

He—a freaking Delta Force operator, one of the country's elite soldiers—had just been outmaneuvered and physically overwhelmed by a woman. And not just any woman, but one whom he outclassed by about a hundred pounds. It was one of the stupidest things he could remember doing in a long, long time.

But it wasn't the unprotected sex that scared him the most. He lay there, letting his heart rate slow down, savoring the sensation of Hannah's body on top of his. He'd never been so aware of a woman before. She smelled like floral shampoo and clean soap. Her breath came in little pants, warming and moistening his neck. Beneath his hands, the skin of her buttocks was as soft and smooth as satin. He could feel her heart thudding hard against his.

He recalled again her expression as she'd eased her body onto his, the sublime pleasure that had transformed her face and riveted his attention.

No, it wasn't the unprotected sex that scared him.

It was how he'd lost control, and how even now, after the most intense orgasm he could ever remember, he was still hard inside her. And wanted to lose control again.

10

SULLY STOOD at the window of his office and stared out over Colombia Avenue. It was a clear day, the kind of crisp, autumn afternoon that beckoned hordes of New Englanders to nearby apple orchards to purchase pumpkins and spiced cider. The kind of day to watch a high-school football game, or take a drive through the White Mountains to see if the leaves had begun to change. It was the kind of day when good things happened, and Sully was feeling very lucky.

He scarcely noticed the flurry of office activity behind him—the ringing of telephones and the layers of conversations, the static interruption of police radios interspersed with the rhythmic hum of a copier machine, or the slamming of a desk drawer.

He'd put in a lot of overtime these past couple of weeks. Of course, nobody knew that his after-hours business primarily entailed shaking down a new liquor store that had opened over on Dorchester Street.

The two brothers who owned it were just a couple of kids, really, but their daily cash intake was in the thousands of dollars. As Sully and his boys had informed the brothers, unless they wanted to use that money for funeral expenses, they'd give up a portion of that income as a goodwill gesture to Craig Cronin. After all, it was only through Cronin's generosity that the boys had even been permitted to purchase the property. It had taken a little persuasion, but the brothers were finally convinced that cutting him in on their lucrative action was definitely in their own best interest.

Yeah, he'd been working some long hours, and he had some time coming to him. He'd ask the captain for a week off, maybe more. Then he'd tell his wife that he was going out of town, that he was following up on an investigation that involved money-laundering and extortion. The irony of it almost made him smile.

Almost.

Looking back toward the central office to ensure nobody was within earshot, he picked up the phone on his desk and punched in a number. He waited until the call was picked up on the other end, and kept his voice low.

"Mick, it's me. No thanks to you, I found the little bitch."

"Who?"

"Whaddya mean, *who?* Hannah Hartwell, that's who. I got a call from some snot-nosed reporter down in North Carolina. Seems my girl is opening up a new shop down there."

"Oh, yeah? Is that what they consider breaking news?" There was no mistaking the sarcasm in Mick's voice. "Shit, Sully, why don't you give it up? You could pay Cronin back—I know you got the money. Just leave the girl alone. It's not like she stole the cash—she probably doesn't even know she has it."

Sully glanced cautiously over his shoulder. "I want that money back."

Mick snorted. "Yeah, twenty-five grand that wasn't yours to start with."

"That was cash I'll have to work hard to replace. Cash that has to come out of my own pockets."

"So why'd this reporter call you?"

"Said he wanted to do a story about her new business, but she ran him off. He did some checking and found out about her un-fortunate experience in South Boston. Said he wanted more in-formation from the arresting officer as to the exact nature of the allegations." Stretching the phone cord as far as it would reach, Sully stepped over to the framed newspaper clipping that showed Hannah being led away in handcuffs. He blew on the glass, dislodging a bit of imaginary dust, and then rubbed the cuff of his shirt across the wood to polish it.

"What did you tell him?"

Sully shrugged, glancing back at the office as he cradled the receiver between his shoulder and chin. "I told him the truth, that the charges didn't stick." He paused. "But the guy's already suspicious. Within two days, everyone in that Podunk town will wonder what she's really selling. That shop won't last a week once word gets out. They'll shut her down so fast, her head will spin."

She'd be sorry she ever said no to him.

"So…what now?"

Sully snorted. "Whaddya think? You, me and a couple of the boys are going on a little road trip. It'll be just like old times."

"Damn, Sully, you think that's a good idea? I mean, she's in fucking North Carolina. How long we going to be gone?"

"As long as it takes to get what she owes me."

"Oh, yeah?" Sully heard the doubt in the other man's voice. "So you get the money back. Then you're gonna leave her alone, right?"

"Yeah, I'll leave her alone," Sully assured him. "Just as soon as she gets what I have for her, and it's been a long time coming."

RANSOM HAD BEEN AWAKE for hours. Hell, he hadn't slept more than an hour all night, and for the first time in weeks, it wasn't a migraine keeping him awake.

He felt better than he had in months. He didn't want to think too much about why. He was a realist. If somebody had told him that his headaches could be relieved through touch, he'd have said they were full of shit. But he had to acknowledge that when Hannah Hartwell touched him, his headaches vanished.

He bent his arms behind his head, careful not to disturb the woman who lay curled against him like a contented kitten, one hand resting over his heart. Her hair spread over his shoulder like a skein of pale, honey-streaked silk and her skin was almost translucent against the suntanned brown of his own. One slim leg was thrown across his thighs, and she was pressed against him from his neck all the way down to his ankles.

He groaned softly and tried not to think of how incredibly soft her body was against his, or how good she smelled, or how he had only to turn his hips slightly to gain access to the sweetest, most intimate part of her.

It was almost four-thirty in the morning, and Hannah had been asleep for several hours. He should have slipped out of her apartment the second her breathing had become slow and regular. He'd had sex with a lot of women, but he couldn't recall the last time he'd actually slept with one.

In her bed.

He never did that, and in doing so, he'd broken one of his own rules. He tried to tell himself that he'd been reluctant to wake her. Trying to untangle himself from her body without disturbing her would have been nearly impossible.

But he knew that was a bunch of crap. If he wanted to, he could extricate himself from a nest of adders without disturbing any of them.

The truth was, he'd wanted to stay.

He couldn't remember ever being with a woman like Hannah. She'd been so sweet, and so giving. So unbelievably hot for him. She'd held nothing back, at least physically, but he couldn't quite shake the sense that while her body had been fully engaged, there was a part of herself that she'd kept hidden from him.

Despite telling himself a thousand times that it didn't matter, he knew he was lying. He wanted to know her secrets. Wanted to share his own with her, and how freaking scary was that? Even the army shrink at Walter Reed hadn't elicited that kind of response from him.

Of course, the psychiatrist who'd been assigned to evaluate him hadn't licked and sucked or otherwise tasted just about every part of his body, either. Amazing how having your dick in someone's mouth inspired a certain amount of trust.

He thought again about the previous night, and the expression on Hannah's face each time he'd brought her to orgasm. He loved how she chewed her lower lip and concentrated, and that her eyes glazed over when she was getting close.

How she panted his name in that soft, broken way as she came apart, and clung to him as if he was her lifeline, her limbs wrapped so tightly around him that he didn't know where he ended and she began.

He'd made her come a half-dozen times, but for once, he hadn't done it as an obligatory prelude to his own release.

He'd genuinely loved watching her unravel. He'd even held off on his own climax to prolong hers and draw it out until she shuddered and looked at him with something like wonder in her blue eyes.

His head told him he should have left hours ago, but his body told a different story altogether. He wanted her again.

Badly.

Admittedly, there didn't seem to be much point in doing a duck-and-evade maneuver now. They lived under the same roof.

There'd be no avoiding her.

Besides, he wasn't all that certain he wanted to end this quite so soon. He'd already promised to help her with the shop, which pretty much ensured they'd be in close proximity for at least the next week or so.

His gaze drifted over Hannah, lingering on the soft fullness of her lips and her flushed cheeks, watching the rhythmic rise and fall of her chest in utter fascination. Her breasts were small, the nipples pale and pink, but they fit perfectly in the palms of his hands.

He closed his eyes and groaned inwardly, knowing he was in

real danger here. She aroused every protective male instinct he had. Hell, she just plain aroused him.

It had been an amazing night. After they'd made love that first time, he'd pulled her into the small bathroom with him. He recalled again how she'd looked standing naked in the shower, with the water sluicing down her body, hands braced against the glass enclosure as he'd knelt before her…and, after he'd lifted her into his arms and carried her out of the shower, how she'd looked sprawled on the bathroom counter, head thrown back as he'd moved between her splayed thighs. He hadn't been able to get enough of her.

As if on cue, she murmured something incoherent, her eyelashes fluttered, and then he was gazing down into the luminous blue of her eyes. Sleepy and bemused, she stared up at him for a moment, and then smiled.

"I'm still dreaming."

"Not unless I'm having the same dream, babe," Ransom said softly, and brushed his knuckles against her cheek.

She continued to watch him, and the sleepy confusion was slowly replaced with an expression of dawning awareness as she came fully awake. She shifted against him, and her eyes widened even more as she felt his stiff cock against the juncture of her thighs.

"Oh, my," she said softly, and reached down to grasp him in her hand. Her slender fingers stroked him. "What a nice way to wake up."

Ransom couldn't agree more, but, damn, they'd already used the two condoms he kept in his wallet. He was determined there'd be no more unprotected sex. The sensation of being inside Hannah, without the latex barrier, had been mind-blowing, but it wouldn't happen again.

"We're out of protection, babe, unless you can wait while I run up to my apartment." Reaching over, he picked his wristwatch up from the bedside table and peered at the illuminated face. "Which probably isn't an option, since I need to be out of here in about fifteen minutes."

"Where do you go so early every morning?"

"Camp Lejeune, darlin'."

"Can't you be late?"

Ransom thought of the consequences. A Delta operator had to be dead not to show up for duty. If he was even a minute late, he could kiss the upcoming mission goodbye.

"Not a chance. And we're down to fourteen minutes, and counting."

Hannah smiled, a slow curving of her lips that promised everything. "We don't need condoms for what I have in mind," she whispered, and stretched upward to kiss him. "And I'm pretty sure I can have you out of here in, oh, about three minutes."

Ransom groaned and buried his hands in her hair, slanting his mouth across her lips and tangling his tongue against hers. She made a soft noise of approval, and Ransom could feel her small breasts brushing over his chest as she continued to fondle him, stroking her hand up and down the length of his erection.

Dragging her mouth from his, she pressed moist kisses along the length of his jaw, and down the side of his neck, lingering briefly over his nipples and then moving lower.

Ransom's stomach muscles contracted when she skated her tongue over his abdomen, and then pulled back slightly to consider his cock.

"Mmm," she hummed. "You look...delicious."

Holding him with one hand, she dipped her head and lightly ran her tongue around the rim of his straining erection.

Ransom's entire body jerked.

She lifted her head, her eyes luminous. "Do you want me to stop?"

Christ. *"No."*

Hannah smiled in satisfaction and bent back to her exploration, wetting his shaft with one long sweep of her tongue and sliding her hand firmly over him. She sank her teeth lightly into the flesh of his thigh, before soothing the area with gentle licks, as she cupped and caressed his sac.

When she took him in her mouth, Ransom's toes curled.

The combination of her soft, wet mouth and the movement of her fingers as they stroked and squeezed him, was enough for him to sink back against the pillows with a ragged groan of surrender.

He wanted to drag her away from his body, spread her across the bed and use his mouth on her until she came in long, shuddering sighs, but she'd sweetly and succinctly wrested all control away from him as no other woman had.

Ever.

Watching her was the most erotic thing he'd ever witnessed, and when she swirled her tongue around the head of his erection, he gritted his teeth. He was close to losing it totally. Right now.

"Hannah. *Wait.*" He was gasping, his hands cupping her face, stroking her long hair back so he could see her, see what she was doing to him. Destroying him completely.

In less than three minutes.

"No, I *want* to." Her voice was muffled around him.

Christ.

He needed to pull away, needed her to pull away, but then she did something with her hands and her tongue, and it was all over for him—he was a goner.

He exploded in a white-hot rush of pleasure that made him groan loudly and collapse back against the mattress, obliterated. He lay there, shocked and gasping, until she came over him on all fours, and stroked her thumb across his lower lip.

"Ransom? Was that…okay?"

He forced himself to focus on her, saw the uncertainty in her blue eyes, and hauled her against him, wrapping his arms tightly around her. His breathing was still ragged.

Jesus, he'd just had the most mind-blowing orgasm of his life, and she was asking if it was *okay*.

"It was…unbelievable."

With a huff of relieved laughter, she turned her face into his neck and pressed her lips against the spot where his pulse still beat unsteadily. "Well, I thought so, too."

"Now it's your turn," he said huskily into her ear, smoothing a hand over the small of her back, where her narrow waist flared into the curve of hip and buttocks. "We still have ten minutes left."

To his surprise, she gave a huge yawn and cuddled closer. "You know what? I think I'm happy right where I am. In fact, I don't want to move. I think another orgasm might kill me." She smiled against his neck, tickling his skin with her breath. "Imagine having to report that to your commanding officer. 'Death by orgasm. Sorry, sir, I killed her with passion. But she went with a smile on her face.'"

"Hannah…" He couldn't let her go to sleep without returning the favor. To do so went against everything in him.

"Shh," she said, laying her cheek on his chest and wrapping her arms around him. "I'm happy. I'm exactly where I want to be. There'll be plenty of time…later. After I've regained my strength. Besides, you need to go."

"Okay," he said reluctantly, knowing she was right. "But I'm insisting on a rain check."

He carefully disentangled himself from her and drew the covers over her nudity. She smiled up at him, and then curled against the pillow and closed her eyes. "Bye," she murmured sleepily.

Ransom hated to leave. As he gathered up his discarded clothing and dressed quickly in the semidarkness, he was completely aware of the woman in the bed. He listened to her breathing deepen. As amazing as it seemed, she'd drifted off, just like that.

He paused at the foot of the bed to watch her sleep, completely humbled and dismayed. He couldn't remember the last time a woman had given him so much pleasure without demanding *something* in return.

In the space of mere hours, Hannah had caused him to break three of his cardinal rules. Never have unprotected sex. Never climax before your partner, and never, *ever* spend an entire night in her bed. He gave a disbelieving huff of laughter. With her sweet, sensual methods, she was turning out to be more dangerous than any insurgent he'd ever come up against.

With her, he wasn't in danger of losing his life; he was in serious danger of losing his heart.

11

THE SOUND OF HAMMERING brought Hannah awake with a violent start. She sat up, heart pounding. Her first conscious thought was that Sully was at her door, pounding his fist on the panels and demanding she let him in.

It took a moment to realize she was alone. And naked. Which brought memories of the previous night rushing back. Relaxing on the pillows, she stretched luxuriously and then winced. She was deliciously tender in places she'd only dreamed of. In fact, if not for those aches, she might have believed the previous night was no more than a figment of her imagination.

But when she turned to check the clock on the bedside table, she saw the note Ransom had left for her, hastily scribbled on the back of an old receipt and propped against the bedside lamp.

Didn't want to wake you. We're in the shop. R.

She frowned.

What time had he left? She couldn't remember, knew only that it had been during the predawn hours. She reread his note.

We're in the shop? Who was he in there with?

The hammering on the other side of the wall became louder, joined by the high whine of what sounded like an electric saw. When the headboard itself actually began to shake from the force of the pounding, Hannah leaped out of the bed, dragging the sheet with her. She stood in the middle of the room, staring at the wall, half expecting it to explode inward at any second.

What in the world…?

If it weren't for the fact that Ransom had left the note saying he was in the shop, she'd be completely freaked out. Okay, even with the note, she was completely freaked out.

But when she glanced at the bedside clock and saw it was past noon, she was galvanized into action. Jeez, a full eight hours had passed since Ransom had left her early that morning. How could she have slept so late? She never slept past seven!

Dragging the sheet with her, Hannah hurried into the bathroom and turned on the shower. Only when she stood beneath the steaming jets of water did she begin to relax and allow herself to think about the previous night.

She still couldn't quite believe she'd had sex with Ransom Bennett. And not just sex—the most amazing sex of her life. She knew without a doubt that if she lived to be a hundred, there would never be another man like him.

He'd drawn her out of herself, made her feel more than she'd ever felt before in her life. And it hadn't been just about the way he'd made her feel, physically. The look in his eyes as he'd watched her come apart had been so intent that she'd been certain he could see into her very soul.

She never would have guessed, after meeting him that first night, that there was a tender, passionate side to the man. But he'd been so careful with her, as if she was a piece of her grandmother's china, liable to break if treated roughly. At the same time, he'd demanded she give herself fully to him, accepting no half measures. He'd pushed her to the brink of what she thought she could bear, and then he'd pushed her even further.

She could still feel his hands on her body, hear his roughened voice in her ears, see the glittering intensity of his stare as he'd completely blown her away.

She'd never had sex with a man that she didn't have some feeling for, at least a little bit. Despite her brave self-talk about using sex as a means to release pent-up frustrations, she'd never been able to sleep with a man strictly for the pleasure his body could provide. But even with an emotional connection, none of those previous lovers had ever made her feel the way Ransom did.

Exposed.

Vulnerable.

As if he could see all the way to her soul.

And despite having made love with him to the point where she'd been bonelessly sated, she realized it wasn't enough.

She wanted more.

Turning off the water, she wrapped a towel around herself and stepped out of the shower, directly into a warm, masculine chest. She gave a small yelp of surprise, only to have a pair of strong arms come firmly around her.

"Easy, it's just me." There was no mistaking the deep voice, with its smoky undertones.

She sagged in relief. "Holy crap, you scared the life out of me."

Ransom bent down to press a kiss against her bare shoulder, his lips curving into a smile. "Sorry, I didn't mean to freak you out. I borrowed the key to the shop, and asked a few buddies from the base to come over and help me out. I didn't think you'd mind."

Her entire body reacted to the sensation of his lips against the side of her neck.

"Consider me officially freaked out," she replied, trying to control the unsteady wobble in her voice. The things he was doing with his hands were completely distracting her.

"I told myself I wouldn't come in," he muttered against her ear, his breath hot. "I wanted you to get some sleep, since you didn't get any last night, but I kept thinking about you. Naked. Alone."

"Uh-huh." She couldn't think straight, especially when he used one finger to part her folds and sink a finger inside her. Her legs went wobbly, and her breath whooshed out of her lungs in one long sweep. "How long have you been in the shop?"

"Not long," he answered, skating his lips along the line of her jaw and using his teeth to tug gently at her earlobe, as his hand worked magic between her legs. "Jesus, you feel good."

Hannah groaned as he used his fingers to swirl her wetness around, sliding his thumb over the nub of her clitoris and nearly lifting her onto her toes.

Ransom picked her up as if she weighed nothing, and strode across the hallway to the bedroom, where he laid her down across the rumpled bed. After the humid warmth of the bathroom, the air was cool enough to raise goose bumps across her flesh, but Hannah scarcely noticed. Heat was building inside her, burning its way through her veins and pulsing urgently between her thighs.

He spread her legs and stared down at her with raw desire in his eyes. It was only then that Hannah saw what he was wearing, and she couldn't stop the little thrill that ran through her.

He was in uniform. Desert camouflage battle dress uniform. His sleeves were rolled up over his bulging biceps, and to Hannah, he seemed even bigger and broader than usual. The military uniform, combined with the scar on his forehead, gave him a dangerous appearance. She shivered.

He looked so damned good, it almost hurt to see him. Instantly, Hannah knew he was someone men would willingly fight alongside. He had a presence, an inherent confidence and a no-kidding attitude that spoke volumes. While she'd known he was a soldier, she hadn't really thought about what that meant, until now.

Then a horrifying thought occurred to her.

"You're not leaving, are you?" she asked, hating that her voice sounded so anxious. "I mean, are you deploying?"

She didn't know anybody who was active-duty military, but she'd seen and read enough news reports to appreciate just how dangerous a deployment to the Middle East could be. The thought of Ransom in danger made her stomach clench.

Never mind that he looked as if he could single-handedly put an end to the conflict over there in about a week.

Now he looked at her sharply. "What?"

"You're in uniform," she pointed out. "I haven't seen you in uniform before. Are you deploying?"

Immediately, his face cleared. "No, babe, I'm not going anywhere."

"Then…"

"I'm in the military, darlin'. This is standard dress code, but I'm more than happy to take it off."

"But I thought you were on medical disability? I mean, your leg…"

"Trust me," he assured her in a silken voice, "I've never felt better."

As if to prove his point, he guided her hand to the hard thrust of his erection beneath the camo trousers.

"I see what you mean," she said breathlessly, and stroked him through the coarse material of the pants.

"Ah, babe," he groaned. "You're all I could think about this morning. I damned near killed myself to get through my morning routine, and get back here."

Hannah felt a warm burst of pleasure at his words. *He'd wanted to see her.*

Beyond the bedroom, the electric saw whined into life once more, reminding Hannah that only a wall separated them from whatever mayhem was occurring in the shop. "What is going on over there?" she asked. "Should I be worried?"

"Only if the noise stops. Christ, you're so damned hot," Ransom muttered, his fingers going to his zipper. His dog tags were hidden beneath his camo shirt and the T-shirt he wore beneath that, but Hannah could imagine how they were nestled against his skin, much the way she wanted to be. Despite the fact he'd gotten little sleep the previous night, he looked rested. But Hannah could see that he was nowhere near relaxed.

His body was so tightly coiled, he seemed ready to detonate, and a muscle jumped in his lean jaw as he raked his gaze over her.

Watching him as he stood at the side of the bed with his hands on his fly, Hannah felt her mouth go dry with anticipation. In another second, he'd release that gorgeous erection she could see straining against his zipper. She grew wet just thinking about having him inside her, and when he reached down and drew a finger along her cleft, she actually whimpered with pleasure.

The high-pitched whine of the electric saw stopped, but less than a second later, someone began hammering against the wall behind the bed. Hannah watched Ransom's face, half expecting him to react to the noise, but he didn't seem at all fazed by it, proof to her that his head injury wasn't an issue. At least not this morning.

His expression as he looked down at her was hot with desire. She'd never felt so beautiful or confident about her own sexuality. If the raw, masculine appreciation in his eyes was anything to go by, the guy was completely and totally turned on. The knowledge was heady stuff.

Lifting her legs, Hannah hooked her toes onto the waistband of his fatigues so that when he unfastened his belt and opened his zipper, she could help pull them down.

The position opened her to his gaze, and when he drew a condom from his back pocket and ripped it open, Hannah could see his hands weren't entirely steady. Shoving his underwear down over his hips, Hannah drank in the sight of his erection, rising rigid and engorged against his abdomen.

"Oh," she sighed, and before he could sheathe himself in the condom, she stroked her finger over the tip, teasing the tiny slit until she had enough lubrication to rub it over the head.

"Hannah," he growled, his face taut, "you're killing me."

"Soldier," she crooned, "you need to toughen up."

But her own hands trembled as she helped him roll the condom down the thick length of his penis and then cupped his sac, caressing him from below and absorbing his small grunts of pleasure.

"Enough," he finally gasped, "or I'm not going to last. Here, under your hips." He grabbed a pillow from the bed and Hannah obediently raised her hips as he pulled her to the very edge of the mattress and positioned it beneath her bottom. "Perfect," he said, his voice thick. "Ah…*there.*"

With one hand on her knee to keep her thighs open, he positioned himself at the entrance to her body and thrust slowly forward.

Hannah stopped breathing.

Behind them, the pounding of a hammer continued.

With excruciating slowness, Ransom gradually filled her, stretching her.

Hannah gasped in pleasure.

Taking her ankles in both his hands, he raised her legs and bent her knees back, opening her for his thrusts.

"Ah…*damn.*" He groaned, and Hannah dragged her eyes from the spot where he was sinking inside her body. His head was back, his teeth clenched, the scar on his forehead standing out in stark relief. The cords in his neck strained as he pumped steadily into her.

The feel of his hard flesh, filling her, then easing out, then filling her again with maddening slowness, was an almost unbearable pleasure. Combined with the erotic vision he made in his uniform, Hannah knew she wasn't going to last.

She breathed his name, feeling an orgasm beginning to build. With his hands holding her ankles, and her fingers fisted in the sheets of the bed, she had no ability to control their pace.

Nor did she want to.

She just wanted to give herself over to this man.

He'd opened his eyes, and now he captured her gaze and held on to it. His expression was taut, all the pleasure he was feeling written clearly across his gorgeous face. It was an incredible turn-on.

The hammering in the adjoining room continued and behind the headboard, the wall trembled.

"Oh, oh..." Her voice low and husky with need, and Ransom's face tightened.

"That's it, babe," he rasped. "Come for me."

Raising one of her legs, he rested her foot on his shoulder, and leaned forward to cup and knead her breasts, first one and then the other. Hannah arched into his hand as he rolled her nipple between his fingers.

But when he smoothed his hand over her belly and swirled his finger over the sensitive rise of flesh above her cleft, she cried out. She was being swept toward something bigger than herself, caught in its strong currents, her body helpless against the powerful pull of pleasure.

Ransom's eyes were locked on hers. "Come on, darlin', take me with you..." Passion added more smoke to his voice, roughened it with need.

So close now.

So.

Close.

Ransom thrust hard and deep, his finger circling the small nub until, suddenly, she was falling, with wave after undulating wave of sensation crashing over her. She convulsed around him, her body clenching his until he also shuddered, groaning his release.

He stood with his head back and eyes closed for a minute, and then the breath went out of him. Turning his face, he pressed a kiss against Hannah's ankle where it still rested on his shoulder, and then lowered her legs.

Hannah realized the hammering had stopped, and there was no sound at all coming from the shop.

"Please tell me your buddies aren't on the other side of that wall with their ears pressed against the plaster," she croaked, when she finally found her voice.

Ransom laughed a little unevenly. "Not if they want to live, they aren't."

Withdrawing from her body, he discarded the condom and readjusted his clothing. Then he scooped Hannah more fully into the center of the bed, before joining her on the mattress, pulling her against his warmth. Raising himself on one elbow, he traced a finger along the line of her collarbone.

"Now we're even," he murmured, and kissed her so sweetly she felt her eyes burn. "Not that I'm keeping score."

She hugged him fiercely, wanting to surround him with her body, to keep him close.

To *keep* him.

Pulling back slightly, Hannah searched his eyes, surprised by what she saw reflected there. She traced the pad of her thumb over his lip, then over the roughness of his jaw. He closed his eyes and made a humming sound of pleasure, as if he savored her touch. Experimentally, she touched her fingers to his scar.

Nothing. Not even a hint of discomfort.

Reading her thoughts, Ransom brought her hand to his mouth and kissed the inside of her palm. "I guess we're going to have to disclose our findings to the medical community, after all," he teased. "Sexual healing really does work."

She ducked her head so he wouldn't see her confusion, and he laughed, mistaking it for embarrassment.

"Hey," he said, putting a finger beneath her chin and tipping her face up. "I'm kidding. This will be our secret, and I hope I'm the only one you'll share your treatments with, although I still can't figure out how you do it. It's like you touch me, and *bam!* Pain's gone. You could make a fortune doing what you do."

Hannah shrugged. "It's a private thing. I don't know where it comes from. I haven't told many people about it, either, mostly because they don't understand. I wish I could explain how it works, but I can't. It's just something I *do*. Like breathing."

She didn't like talking about her unique ability—she'd spent most of her life trying to hide it. Through Reiki, she'd finally been able to bring it out into the open and put it to some practical use, but there were still people out there who thought she was a complete whacko.

"It's okay," he murmured, bending his forehead to hers. "We don't have to talk about it if you don't want to. And you don't have anything to prove to me, darlin'. I'm a believer."

She raised her eyes to his, and his expression was warm enough to make her toes curl. "Really?"

"Really."

Flustered, she focused on the broad chest in front of her, and ran her fingers over the black insignia stitched into his camo shirt.

"So what are you, a general or something?"

He laughed softly. "Ah, the lady wants to change the subject. Sorry, darlin'. Not even close. I'm a chief warrant officer."

"Oh." She had no idea what that was, or where it fell in the military hierarchy. "Sounds important."

"Nah. We're a dime a dozen."

Not true.

Hannah knew in her heart there was nobody else out there like Ransom Bennett.

"So what do you do, exactly?"

"Exactly?"

"Yeah. Do you drive a tank? Are you a sniper, or some kind of explosives expert? I don't know much about the military, so it's all pretty much a mystery to me. It's just that I know so little about you, and after last night…and this morning, well, it would be nice to get to know each other a little better."

He picked up a tendril of her damp hair and twirled it lazily around one finger. "In case you haven't noticed, darlin', you're lying here buck naked. I think that pretty much qualifies us as good friends."

Hannah blushed but refused to relinquish the subject. "Can you at least tell me how you were injured? Were you in Iraq?"

"Sorry. That's classified."

She pursed her lips and considered him. "Are all military guys this secretive?"

Ransom just laughed. "Okay, I surrender. What do you want to know? I was born and raised here in North Carolina, and the army has been the one constant in my life. I like old cars and high-tech gadgets, and my favorite color is—"

"Green. I know." She ran her hand over the breast of his camouflage shirt with a smile. "What about your family? You said your father was career army."

"Yep, he was. Airborne Ranger." Hannah heard the pride in his voice. "He retired about ten years ago, but I think he still misses the army. He was gone more than he was home, which I'm pretty sure contributed to the end of his marriage. Even so, I wanted to be just like him when I grew up. I couldn't wait for the day when I could finally join the military."

"I'm sure he's very proud of you." Hannah slid her arms around him, hugging him tight. "Do you ever see your mom? I mean after she left…"

Ransom made a shrugging motion. "I see her every once in a while. She's pretty much moved on with her life, though. I don't think she was ever cut out to be an army wife or a mother."

Hannah made a sound of sympathy, and he pressed a kiss against her brow. "It's okay, I've accepted it."

"Where does your dad live now?"

"He's over in Fayetteville. He's been with the same woman now for about eight years. My younger brother lives a few miles away, with his wife and little girl."

His voice changed as he talked about his brother's family,

taking on a warm, affectionate tone that Hannah had never heard before.

"You have a niece."

"Oh, yeah." There was no mistaking the smile in his voice. "Little Piper. She's four years old, and has every male in the family wrapped around her tiny finger, including me."

Hannah's chest tightened, and she recognized the sensation as jealousy. More than anything, she wanted to hear that warmth and affection in his voice when he talked about her.

"Ah," she teased, "so your biggest secret is out. You're a complete sucker for cute little girls."

He laughed and stood up, pulling her to her feet. "Yes, I am. As you very well know. Listen, babe, I hate to leave, but I should go next door and check things out." He pressed a brief, hard kiss to her lips. "And something tells me I'm not the only one with secrets, darlin'."

12

"THERE'S MORE to your little lady friend than what's in this file," Alec Carvotti said, handing a large, brown envelope to Ransom. "As far as I'm concerned, this is just preliminary data. I'm running a check on a guy who gave her some trouble back in Boston and I should have more for you tomorrow."

Christ. His instincts had been right.

There was something in Hannah's background that wasn't good, and suddenly Ransom wasn't all that sure he wanted to know what that something was.

He could change his mind. He could hand the envelope back to Alec. The dossier and whatever information it contained would disappear.

They stood in the back room of Hannah's shop, where the rest of the unit was putting the finishing touches on the remodeling that she'd requested. And, okay, they'd done a little more than she'd asked, but she didn't need to know about the security camera that Ransom had installed in the ceiling fan, that was triggered via a motion detector. Neither did she need to know about one they'd mounted over the front entry.

Ransom told himself it wasn't Hannah he didn't trust—it was everyone else. If she was going to run the business by herself, he'd make sure she at least had some protection. It was just an added safety measure for when he couldn't be there to personally watch over her.

He took the file from Alec and turned it over in his hands. It wasn't very thick, but he knew it contained everything he'd ever need to know about Hannah Hartwell. Probably more information than even her closest friends or family knew about her. He'd asked for the dossier. So why did he suddenly find himself so reluctant to look at it?

"Hey, man," Alec said, reading his thoughts. "Nobody says you have to read it. I know that everything we do, every decision we make, is based on reconnaissance and intelligence-gathering, and educated assumptions. But that's the job, man. It's not real life."

"The way I see it, there's no difference."

Alec's expression was wry. "You know, you could actually go into this relationship like every other sorry son of a bitch out there, and just wing it. Nothing says you have to know all her secrets." He waggled his eyebrows meaningfully. "At least not the first week."

Ransom slapped the envelope lightly against the palm of his hand. "Thanks for this. I know what you're saying, and I appreciate it, but I believe in the adage of *trust but verify.*"

Alec shrugged. "It's your call, Chief. But if you're going to read it, I'd do it sooner than later. It makes for a helluva bedtime story."

"Hey, Chief?"

Both Ransom and Alec turned to see Conor McCallum standing in the doorway of the small room. His expression was unreadable as he stepped forward and handed a packet to Ransom.

"I was moving that display case when a little door underneath opened up and this fell out."

Ransom turned the packet over in his hands. It was a large manila envelope that bulged at the seams, secured with several rubber bands. He glanced at Conor.

"You've looked at what's in here."

"Yep."

Slowly, his heart growing heavier with each movement, Ransom slid the rubber bands from the envelope and lifted the flap. For a moment he stared at the money inside, and then riffled it with his thumb. He guessed there was more than twenty grand inside the envelope.

Over his shoulder, Alec let out a low whistle. "Shit. That's a lot of dead presidents."

Ransom drew in a breath and let it out slowly. He wouldn't jump to conclusions. If his military training had taught him one thing, it was never to make assumptions. But he couldn't come up with a single reason Hannah would have so much cash stashed away in the bottom of a display cabinet, and not deposited safely in an interest-earning account.

"Man, forget about what I just said. I think you really need to read that dossier," Alec said quietly.

TWENTY MINUTES LATER, Hannah stood just inside the open door to her shop, unable to close her mouth.

Two men dominated the small room. Hard-muscled, hard-eyed, capable men who obviously spent enough time in each other's company to trade good-natured insults with ease. But even more amazing, they'd transformed the two-room shop into a space she scarcely recognized.

The smell of fresh paint was strong. Shelving units had been built into the walls where she'd wanted them; a ceiling fan rotated lazily in the center of the room, and one of the men stood on a ladder near the reception counter, installing recessed lighting, while the second man handed him pieces and parts.

"Holy crap."

She wasn't aware she'd said the words out loud until both men swiveled their gazes in her direction. Despite their casual jeans and T-shirts, their postures were alert. In the instant that their eyes swept over her, Hannah sensed they might even be dangerous.

"Good morning, ma'am." The man at foot of the ladder nodded his head in her direction. "You must be Hannah."

Hannah smiled uncertainly and stepped toward him, extending her hand. "I can't believe this. It's like a miracle. I've been wondering how on earth I was ever going to whip this place into shape by the end of next week, and it seems you've already accomplished it."

"All in a day's work," he said, and a smile split his features, making him look about fifteen years old. He had auburn eyes and bright, blue eyes, and his face was covered in freckles. Despite his wholesome, boy-next-door image, Hannah had the distinct sense that he wasn't a man you wanted to mess with. He enfolded her hand in his, sweeping his gaze over her in appreciation. "I'm Conor, and the guy on the ladder is Jeb."

Jeb looked down at her, his dark eyes missing nothing. His hair was black and shiny as a raven's wing. His skin was gorgeous, smooth and coppery. The thrust of his cheekbones, combined with the slash of his black eyebrows and proud nose told her he was Native American. Hannah wasn't certain, but she thought she saw mistrust and maybe even censure in his narrowed eyes.

He inclined his head briefly in her direction. "Ms. Hartwell," he said, before returning his attention to the canister light overhead, dismissing her.

"Ransom's in the other room," the first man said, angling a disgusted look at Jeb. "We're just about finished here, so we should be out of your hair shortly."

Hannah stared around her, hardly able to comprehend the transformation the men had achieved. The walls glowed a rich, deep terra-cotta with the new coat of paint they'd applied. Even the woodwork and the shelving units sported a fresh layer of white paint.

What they'd done in the back room was even more astounding. The wall-to-wall carpeting had been removed, exposing the beautiful hardwood flooring beneath. Here, the walls were painted a soothing shade of blue-green. On the opposite side of the room, floor-to-ceiling shelving had been installed, and Hannah understood the source of the hammering she'd heard against her bedroom wall.

Ransom and another man stood on the far side of the room, wrestling wooden plantation shutters over the windows that faced Mike Howard's house.

"Good morning," she said, crossing the room toward them. "What a transformation! I can't believe this is the same place. It's amazing."

They had moved her boxes into this room and stacked them neatly against the wall near the door. A large brown envelope lay on the box nearest her, and she automatically reached for it, thinking that Ransom or one of the other men must have brought her mail in from outside.

Before she could pick it up, however, Ransom was there, neatly withdrawing the envelope from her reach. But not before she'd seen the words stenciled across the front: *CW3 Bennett—Eyes Only.*

"Sorry," he said. "I left that there."

Hannah watched as he folded it in half and shoved it into a deep pocket on the side of his camo pants. The man by the window shot a swift glance between her and Ransom, and then returned his attention to the shutters.

An uncomfortable feeling uncoiled itself low in her belly.

Something was wrong.

Hannah had sensed it as soon as Ransom looked at her. She'd taken extra care with her appearance, and knew she looked good, but there was no appreciative gleam in Ransom's eyes. In fact, if they hadn't made love less than an hour earlier, she might actually feel awkward.

He avoided her gaze, and when he did look at her, it was if she was a stranger to him, and not the woman he'd held in his arms and loved so thoroughly just that morning. His demeanor was courteous but cool.

Yep, those were definitely negative vibes she was picking up from him, and awkward didn't begin to describe how she was starting to feel.

"Is everything all right?"

Maybe it was something related to his job.

Ransom seemed to gather his self-composure, and, okay, that was a sort-of smile curving his mouth, but it didn't come close to reaching his eyes.

"Uh, yeah, everything's fine. Absolutely."

Hannah looked sharply at him. His words said one thing, but his body language said something else.

Something was up.

But if Ransom could pretend that nothing was wrong, then so could she. "This really is amazing," she repeated with an expansive gesture toward the room. "I can't believe what you've done in such a short time. I'm just overwhelmed."

The man by the window turned around, glancing between herself and Ransom. "It was no big deal," he assured her. "Ran said he had a friend who needed a hand, so here we are." He set down the electric drill he was holding and extended his hand. "He just didn't say how pretty you are. I'm Billy Pagan. Pleasure to meet you."

He was younger than Ransom, with an outrageously flirtatious gleam in his gray eyes, and Hannah found herself responding to his overt friendliness.

"Okay, let's get this last shutter on, and then you guys are done here," Ransom said, giving Billy a meaningful look.

Unfazed, Billy continued to grin at Hannah. "Sure, Chief."

"I'm not kidding. You've got ten minutes, and then you're out of here, finished or not."

With a wink at Hannah, Billy picked up the electric drill and turned back to what he'd been doing. "I'm a total chick magnet, and the chief knows it. He can't handle the competition."

Before Hannah could respond, another man entered the room, coming to an abrupt halt when he saw her. He stood in the doorway for a moment, his focus moving between Hannah and Ransom, before he quickly made a decision.

Stepping toward Hannah, he put his hand out to her. "Good morning, ma'am. You must be Ms. Hartwell."

Jeez. Did they all know who she was? It was a little unnerving.

"I'm Alec Carvotti," he continued. "I hope you like what we've done with the place, but if not, just say the word and we'll redo it."

He was totally serious, Hannah could see it in his dark stare. If she gave any indication that their work was less than acceptable, they'd tear it all out and begin again.

"I love what you've done," she assured him. "Really."

He nodded his head and then turned his attention to Ransom. "I, um, have some additional information regarding that new asset you recently, um, acquired. You might be interested in it."

"Fine."

Ransom's voice was flat. Expressionless.

"But if today isn't a good time to review the acquisition history, then we can do it tomorrow morning."

Ransom sighed and rubbed a hand over the back of his neck. "You think I should see it sooner than later."

"I do."

"Okay, fine. How about right after lunch?"

"Sounds good. I'll meet you back at the base at fifteen hundred hours."

Hannah might not have thought anything of the exchange, if Billy hadn't looked up and darted a quick glance between the two men and her. But when he realized she'd caught the furtive look, he bent quickly back to his task of fitting the shutters into the window frame.

Suddenly, Hannah felt distinctly de trop. Whatever they were talking about clearly wasn't meant for her ears, and she thought of the folder that lay in Ransom's pocket.

She didn't know much about the military, but she knew that the cryptic words stamped on the front of the envelope meant that the contents were intended for Ransom's eyes only.

She chewed her lip and pretended to examine the overhead ceiling fan, as if she wasn't listening to their conversation. As if it held absolutely no interest for her.

"I'll be there," Ransom assured him, his voice layered with meaning.

Sliding a sideways glance at the two men, Hannah had the distinct feeling that they were talking in code. Clearly, it was her presence in the room that prevented him from discussing the issue.

"I can wait outside," she offered. "I mean, if it's a matter of national security or something, I wouldn't want to get in the way of that."

She'd meant it as a joke, but when Ransom's eyes flew to hers, she saw something flash in their depths. Regret? Guilt? It was gone before she could tell.

"No, it's fine," he said. "We're doing a standard inventory history of some army property that recently came in. No big deal. In fact—" he checked his watch "—it's getting pretty late. Why don't we grab a quick bite to eat while these guys clean up and clear out?"

She gave him a nod, relieved. Maybe she was reading more into the situation than she should. Maybe it really was just some boring army inventory.

But she didn't miss the quick exchange of looks among the three men, and knew right then that whatever they were talking about had nothing to do with army property.

"Okay," she agreed brightly. "Sounds good."

Putting his hand at the small of her back, he scooped up a

manila envelope from a nearby shelf, and steered her toward the front of the shop. Jeb and Conor were testing the recessed lights, and Hannah paused to watch.

"Well, I guess that about does it," Conor said. "Is there anything else you needed done, ma'am?"

Hannah gestured helplessly. "No. I mean, you've already done more than I could ever wish for." She glanced over at Ransom. "How much do I owe you for doing this? For both the materials and the labor? I mean, it's a Saturday, and I'm sure you guys have better things to do than come over and spruce up my little shop."

Conor and Jeb gave each other a meaningful look, before turning away to clear their tools from the counter.

"Don't worry about it," Ransom replied, but his voice had a hard edge to it. "I'm sure you don't have a lot of cash just lying around, or you'd have hired someone, right? Besides, you've already repaid me, and then some."

What?

She stared at him, hoping he didn't mean what she thought he meant.

"Now wait a minute," she began. "I'm not sure I like what you're implying."

"Let's take this somewhere a little more private," he said in a low voice, and steered her out of the shop and toward his Land Rover.

Opening the passenger door, he helped her in. She scooted onto the seat, but put one hand on the door to prevent him from closing it.

"If you dare suggest that what happened last night is a form of repayment," she said in a low, indignant voice, "I swear, I'll hit you so hard, your headache will *never* go away."

"Relax. Our deal was that you'd give me treatments and I'd help you with your shop." His dark eyes were unfathomable. "The sex...well, that's something else."

No kidding. Totally, amazingly something else.

But the tone of his voice made her uneasy, so she didn't voice her thoughts. Instead, she clamped her lips together as he closed the door. They had already established the fact that neither of them was looking for a long-term, meaningful relationship. Did he think she was going to renege on that part of their deal?

She watched him as he came around to the driver's side and pulled himself up behind the wheel, tossing the manila envelope onto the backseat. Mere inches away from her, in the confined space of the cab, his presence was overwhelming, the sheer maleness of him assailing her senses.

He turned toward her on the bench seat and slid one arm along her seat back as he craned to see through the rear window and reverse out of the driveway. Hannah had only to turn her face and her lips would brush along the smooth bulge of his bicep where it rested on the back of the seat. Suddenly, more than anything, she wanted to kiss him.

She shot a quick glance at his face, hoping he couldn't read her thoughts, but his attention was focused on his driving. He'd said they had a deal, but she realized she didn't care about getting the shop up and running. All she could think was that she *did* want to renege on their deal.

All she wanted was Ransom.

In his arms.

In his bed.

In his life.

"Have you been to the Sea Star Café before?" he asked, as he put the Range Rover into gear and accelerated slowly down the street.

"Um, no, I don't think so," she said, but her attention had shifted to Mike Howard's house. A curtain moved in one of the second-story windows, and she couldn't be sure, but she thought she caught a glimpse of Mike, binoculars in hand. But he wasn't looking in the direction of Hannah's shop. Instead, he had the field glasses trained toward the end of the street, in the direction they were headed.

"What is it?" Ransom followed her gaze, ducking his head to peer through the windshield at Mike's house.

"I thought I saw Mike with his binoculars, but I can't figure out what he's looking at." She turned her direction toward the street, with its mix of houses and commercial storefronts. "It's pretty quiet."

"Yeah, it is," Ransom agreed, but something in his voice made her look sharply at him.

He was staring intently into the side mirror of the Range Rover. Hannah swiveled in her seat to look back through the rear window. The tree-lined street behind them was empty, with several cars parked along the curb. There wasn't anyone on the sidewalk, and she frowned in puzzlement.

"What are you looking at?"

Dragging his gaze from the mirror, Ransom looked over at her and gave her a brief, hard smile. "Nothing you need to worry about."

Okay...

Far from reassuring her, his words made her heartbeat kick up a notch. His eyes had flicked to his rearview mirror to stare at the road behind them, and Hannah shivered at the coldness in them.

RANSOM COULDN'T STOP thinking about the two cars he'd seen parked near the end of the street. They were both rental cars, but that wasn't what he'd found disturbing. The coastal community of Cliftondale, with its oceanside golf courses, quaint shopping district and five-star restaurants, drew tourists from around the country.

Nope, it hadn't been the cars that had caught his attention, but the men sitting inside, trying hard to appear invisible as Ransom had driven past.

Outwardly, he hadn't so much as glanced in their direction,

but he'd gotten a good look at them nonetheless. He didn't like what he'd seen. Two men had occupied the first car, and three more sat in the second. They'd been tough-looking men.

Men with a purpose.

They'd studiously turned their attention to a map as he'd driven past in his Range Rover, but he hadn't missed how they'd flung the maps aside once they thought he was out of sight. He might have believed them to be FBI agents, or undercover cops, but every instinct in his body told him otherwise.

The men he'd seen were thugs, and Ransom was pretty sure that whatever purpose had brought them to Cliftondale, it was outside the law. Worse, he had a gut feeling that it involved Hannah.

"What are you thinking about?"

The soft question jerked him back to the present, to the small table he shared with Hannah, overlooking a narrow stretch of beach. The overhead umbrella protected them from the bright sun. A warm breeze wafted in from the ocean, lifting Hannah's hair from her shoulders and rippling the fabric of her turquoise sundress.

Her blue eyes were filled with concern as she watched him. He'd been holding a salt shaker, absently transferring it from one hand to the other as his mind played through all the possible reasons those men might be in Cliftondale.

On his street.

Watching his house.

He was acutely aware of the bulky manila envelope that lay on the table by his elbow and the brown envelope in the side pocket of his camo pants. The second envelope contained the secrets of Hannah's past and, he was pretty sure, the reason for the men's appearance. Everything in him wanted to open the dossier and read it, especially given Alec's insinuation that he would learn why Hannah had money hidden in her shop.

In the end, however, he hadn't opened the file. He'd thought of Hannah, with her sweet smile and trusting nature, and he hadn't been able to read the dossier. Alec had suggested he go into the relationship without knowing all her secrets. In that moment, Ransom had realized he *did* want a relationship with Hannah. A real relationship with commitments and everything else that went with it. What he couldn't do, however, was start that relationship with mistrust. As much as it went against his nature to walk blindly into a situation, he would trust Hannah.

He looked at her now. With her silky blond hair and big blue eyes, she was the epitome of sweetness. Was it all an act?

He set the salt shaker down on the table with a small thunk. They'd found an outside table on the deck of the Sea Star Café, and had ordered lunch—a burger for himself and some kind of fancy salad for Hannah. She'd ordered a raspberry iced tea, and while he'd have liked a beer or a stiff drink, he hadn't wanted anything that might dull his senses.

"Listen, Hannah," he began, placing both hands on the table. "We need to talk."

She swallowed hard, and Ransom didn't miss the alarm that flared briefly in her eyes before she firmly squelched it.

"It's okay," she said, and gave him such a gentle, understanding smile, that Ransom felt his chest constrict. "I know you're not looking for something permanent, and I just want you to know that I'm okay with it."

What?

His bemusement must have shown on his face. She stared at him for a full minute before hot color spread up her neck. "I thought you were about to give me the brush-off," she mumbled.

"No." The single word came out more emphatically than he'd intended, but it had the desired effect; her face immediately cleared. Ransom pushed down the guilt that surged through him, knowing he was about to wipe that hopeful smile right off her face.

"Oh. Well, that's good, then." Her smile faded as she watched Ransom's face and chewed her bottom lip. "So if it's not us, then I'm guessing it has something to do with that envelope in your pocket."

There was so much trepidation in her voice that it was all Ransom could do not to reach across the table and haul her into his arms. He glanced around the small restaurant, filled mostly with tourists and couples. Behind Hannah, the reflection of the sun on the water was nearly blinding.

Reaching down, he pulled the envelope from his pant pocket and laid it on the table between them, flattening it with his hands.

"What is it?" Her voice was nearly inaudible.

"It's a dossier." Ransom forced himself to meet her eyes.

"A dossier," she repeated blankly. "As in, a private file about someone? With all the details of their life?"

"Yeah."

He could see her struggle to understand and, failing, raised her eyes to his in silent appeal.

"Take a look at it," he said gruffly, and pushed the envelope toward her. He picked up the bulky packet from where it lay between them on the small table and turned it over in his hands before setting it down beside the thinner brown envelope. "Then, when you're finished, explain this."

With her eyes on him, she selected the slender envelope first. The top was sealed, and with a questioning look, she carefully opened it.

Ransom drew in a deep, hard breath, knowing this could very well be the moment when he lost her.

OPENING THE ENVELOPE, Hannah peeked inside to see a thin file. With a feeling of dread, she slid the folder halfway out of the envelope. There, printed across the top in red stenciling, she saw her name.

Underneath that were her social security number and birth date, stamped in the same red letters. A wave of heat washed over her, making her feel weak and ill. Her vision blurred and her heart began to beat so fast she thought it might explode out of her chest.

She couldn't look at Ransom.

Why would he have a file with *her* name on it? With shaking fingers, she slid the slim folder back into the envelope. She had no desire to see the contents.

"I don't understand." Her voice sounded strange, low and shaking.

Reaching out, Ransom took the envelope from her and pushed the manila one toward her. His eyes were dark.

Unfathomable.

When he didn't say anything, she leaned forward and picked up the bulky envelope and opened it. She gasped, her gaze flying to Ransom.

"What is this?"

"That's what I'd like to know. Conor found it stashed inside your display case." His eyes narrowed. "You've never seen this before?"

Hannah gave a choked laugh. "No. I mean, don't you think I'd have bought shades for my windows if I had cash like this lying around? Jeez!"

"How long have you owned the cabinet?"

Hannah flipped through the bills. "I bought it at an auction about three years ago. To think all that time…"

"So you're saying the money isn't yours."

Hannah shook her head, unable to keep the regret out of her voice. "It's definitely not mine. The question is, who *does* it belong to? Actually, no…forget I asked," she said slowly. "I think I have an idea. And I know what that other folder is. You had a background check done on me, didn't you? What I want to know is why?"

Ransom scrubbed a hand over his face, and when he looked at her, there was no mistaking the resignation and regret in his eyes. "I know it looks bad. But if it's any consolation to you, I haven't read the file. Alec gave it to me this morning, but damned if I could bring myself to open it."

"But...*why? Why* would you have a background check done on me?"

Ransom muttered an oath. Leaning back in his chair, he rubbed a hand hard across the back of his neck. When he finally looked at her, his expression was so full of raw emotion that Hannah's heart constricted.

"You want to know why?" he asked softly. "Because I can't stop thinking about you. You've gotten under my skin in a way that no other woman ever has." He leaned over the table and, to her astonishment, cupped her face in his hands. "I wanted—no, I needed—to know everything about you. So...I ran a background check."

Hannah pushed his hands away and stared at him. His words reverberated through her, made her want to dismiss the background check as insignificant.

He couldn't stop thinking about her.

She forced herself to think rationally, to concentrate on what he'd done and not what he said.

"What kinds of things did you want to know? Why wouldn't you *ask* me, instead of launching some kind of investigation?"

"Because I didn't think you'd tell me. Not when it's pretty clear you've been hiding something from me—"

"So you decided to just invade my privacy?" She pressed her fingers to her temples, where her blood throbbed, unable to comprehend what he had done. "You can't just do that... There are laws about that kind of thing."

Ransom pressed his lips together. "Look, I'm not asking you to understand, but if it makes any difference, I'd already decided that I'd rather have you tell me about yourself than read about it in a dossier."

A dossier. Like something out of a James Bond movie.

She stared at him, realizing she knew absolutely nothing about this man. When she finally spoke, she couldn't keep the wobble from her voice.

"You sit there, talking to me about keeping secrets and withholding information, like I'm the one who's done something wrong. But you're really the one who's keeping secrets. You're not just a regular army infantry guy, are you?"

He hesitated. "No."

The waitress chose that moment to bring their food, and they both sat back while she placed a steaming burger and fries in front of Ransom, and a crisp salad topped with grilled shrimp in front of Hannah.

She couldn't eat a bite. She'd be lucky if she didn't get sick. Ransom didn't seem to be doing much better. He squirted some ketchup on his plate but made no move to eat.

"So what are you, like a CIA operative, or something?"

Ransom's regard was steady. "I'm with Special Forces. That's all I can tell you."

Hannah's eyes widened. Even she'd heard of Special Forces, and although she didn't know all that much about them, she knew they represented an elite cadre of soldiers, specially trained for dangerous, covert missions. "Is that how you were injured? Doing a mission for Special Forces?"

"Yeah."

"And you have unlimited access to people's personal information?"

Ransom's lips compressed into a thin line. "Normally, we only compile personal data when it's directly related to an operation. I overstepped my bounds with you."

Damned right.

"It's just—" He looked at her, his eyebrows pulled together as he struggled to explain. "After that first night in the shop, when we—"

"I remember," Hannah interrupted him, feeling hot color wash into her face. She glanced around them, hoping their conversation couldn't be overheard.

She didn't need him to remind her of the night in her shop, when he'd put his mouth on her through her clothing. She spent way too much time recalling that sensual encounter in minute detail, as it was.

A small smile curved his lips as he saw her blush. "After that night, I knew I was in danger."

Hannah stared at him, and something small and bright began to swell in her chest. Her voice, when she spoke, was no more than a husky whisper.

"In danger of what?"

"In danger of being completely distracted by a woman whom I knew nothing about, a woman who obviously didn't *want* me to know too much about her."

"So you had a background check done on me."

"Try to understand," he said softly. Hannah didn't protest when he reached across the table and caught her hand loosely in his. "I've seen the ugliest side of human nature. With the exception of the guys in my unit, I guess I'm not very good at trusting people."

"So what did you think a background check would reveal about me?"

He made a rueful face. "When I saw the indent on your finger where you used to wear a ring, I was pretty sure you'd left a husband behind."

"Like your mother did." Hannah's voice was little more than a whisper.

He shrugged, noncommittal, but it was there on his face.

"That's still not an excuse for what you did."

"No," Ransom agreed quietly. "It's not." He picked the envelope up from where he'd tossed it on the table, and handed it to her. "It's yours. I don't want to see it." Hannah set the envelope of cash down and took the dossier from him again. Opening it, she swiftly read through the contents, amazed at the level of detail. Her entire life—all twenty-five years of it—had been condensed to six pages.

Hannah closed the folder. "This is, um, pretty impressive."

"Is it?"

"Oh, yes. And if you read it, you'll find out all kinds of stuff about me. Even things I wouldn't really care for you to know. Things I wouldn't want anyone to know. Embarrassing things."

His eyebrows pulled together. "We all have those things in our past."

"Yes, but even with all the information your people managed to gather, this file still doesn't tell you anything about *me*."

He frowned. "Come again?"

She placed the file in his hands. "This file isn't me, Ransom. It's a compilation of facts and events, but it's not *me*. There's only one way to really get to know a person, and that's the old-fashioned way."

Ransom hesitated then rolled his shoulders, as if easing a strain. "Here's the thing," he said slowly. "I've never gone into any…situation…without having all the facts in front of me beforehand. It's what I do, and I'm good at it." He looked at her, and there was stark vulnerability in his eyes. "Now you're asking me to fly by the seat of my pants."

Hannah felt something in her chest shift, and thought she understood what he was talking about. He was a man accustomed to making decisions based on information, not on emotions.

Everything he did was carefully planned, each contingency considered and accounted for. She could relate, because she had a tendency to make decisions based on raw emotion and instinct, rather than on facts or sound judgment.

"I'm just asking you to trust me," she finally said.

Ransom reached across the table and lifted her hand from where it lay in her lap, to turn it over thoughtfully in his own.

"Okay," he said at last. "Do what you want with the dossier. Destroy it, if you'd like. I really don't want to know what's in that file. If it's okay with you—if you think you can give me another chance—I'm kinda looking forward to getting to know you the old-fashioned way."

Hannah swallowed hard, and she couldn't meet his eyes. He hadn't said he'd trust her, but he wasn't going to read the file.

That was a start.

"There is one thing that I should probably tell you." She laced their fingers together. His hand was so much larger than hers, his palm callused and warm. The realization that he was with Special Forces gave her some courage. What had happened to her in Boston was probably nothing compared to the things he'd seen and done.

"You don't have to tell me," he said, squeezing her hand.

"No, I want to." She drew in a deep breath. "It could explain where the money came from. You're right when you said I was hiding some things from you. There are things about me that I didn't want you know. Things I'd rather not have anyone know. I'm afraid when you find out—you'll think less of me."

"Darlin'," he said in that warm, smoky voice, a smile curving his lips, "now that I know you don't have a husband out there, I'm pretty sure there isn't anything you could tell me that would make me think less of you."

Hannah gave him a swift, grateful smile. "Yes, well, hold on to that thought." She closed her eyes briefly to gather her courage, then blurted the words out before she could change her mind. "I had a Reiki practice in Boston. Until I was arrested on charges of selling sex out of my shop."

13

RANSOM TURNED incredulous eyes on her. *"What?"*

He watched as Hannah's face flushed red. She caught her lower lip between her teeth and gave a jerky nod of her head.

"It's true. When I was living in Boston, my shop was vandalized. The cop who responded to the call was really nice, and we became friends." She looked at Ransom, her expression earnest. "I know now he would have liked for us to be more than just friends, but he didn't interest me. At least not that way."

"Go on." His voice was grim.

"I began hearing rumors about him, that he was involved with the mob, but I didn't believe it. I mean, he was a *police officer.* He began coming around the shop more often, and he'd say things that made me uncomfortable, but there was no way to avoid him, short of closing the shop."

Ransom was silent. He had to splay his hands on his thighs to keep them from forming into fists. He didn't know who the cop was, but he could picture him clearly. Big. Arrogant. Swaggering.

Hannah played with the stirrer in her drink. "He took me by surprise one day, when I was alone in the back room of the shop. He tried to pressure me into—into—" She broke off, color flooding her cheeks.

Ransom's voice was hard. "He tried to pressure you into having sex with him."

Tight anger uncoiled in his chest. The thought of any man trying to coerce Hannah into having sex made his gut twist.

She was his.

He couldn't think of her with another man without a surge of jealousy so intense that his hands shook. He didn't know who the cop was, but he'd damned well find out. Nothing pissed him off faster than somebody who abused a position of authority.

Like he had when he'd requested the background check on Hannah.

Drawing in a deep breath, he forced himself to speak in a low voice. "What did you do?"

Hannah swallowed hard, and it was all Ransom could do not to pull her into his arms. A silky strand of hair fell across her forehead and over one eye, and he slowly reached over to brush it away.

She turned her gaze toward him, and he could see tears shimmering in her big, take-me-to-bed blue eyes.

"Ah, babe," he groaned, and couldn't resist pressing a kiss into her palm, uncaring of the other patrons who sat at the surrounding tables. "It's going to be okay."

She nodded and gave him a tremulous smile. "I know."

"You told him to get lost."

"Yeah, I did. That's when he started getting nasty. He said he'd have me brought up on charges of selling sex out of my shop unless I agreed to…"

Her voice trailed off.

Now there was no question about what he was going to do. He'd hunt the bastard down and give him an old-fashioned lesson in justice.

"You couldn't even go to the police, because this son of a bitch was on the inside," he guessed.

"Yes. He had me arrested, Ransom."

Her voice broke and Ransom felt something inside him snap.

"On what grounds?"

"He said he'd been watching my business for several weeks, and became suspicious when most of my clients were male, which wasn't true. But he actually had men come forward who said they'd testify to the fact that they'd paid for—for—"

"For sexual services," Ransom finished grimly.

"I hired a lawyer, but he said it would be my word against that of a law enforcement officer and nobody would believe me."

"He was probably right. Tell me the rest."

"I went to court, but the judge threw the case out based on a lack of evidence."

Ransom's fingers tightened around hers, but he didn't say anything. Anyone with eyes in their heads could see how innocent Hannah was. She'd be incapable of selling herself for money. Her fingers clutched his a little convulsively. "You and my lawyer are the only ones who know the truth."

"You didn't do anything wrong," he said roughly.

Hannah eyed him sharply. "Maybe not, but it only confirmed my parents' belief that I should close the business and get a 'real' job. They always said my abilities would bring me trouble, and it seems they were right."

There was no mistaking the bitterness in her voice.

Ransom couldn't stop the wry smile that twisted his lips. "News flash, Hannah. Your abilities had nothing to do with it."

At her startled expression, he threaded his fingers with hers. "I don't need to read the dossier to know this creep took one look at you and decided he had to have you. And when he realized he couldn't have you, he decided to destroy you, instead. Your parents are just trying to protect you."

Hannah gave him a tremulous smile. "I'm not so sure that's true. If you *had* read the file, you'd have learned my father is the founder and CEO of Hartwell Industries. He's always concerned about negative publicity."

"*Jesus*. The oil-and-gas-exploration firm?"

"Yep."

Ransom couldn't believe it. Hartwell Industries was world renowned. The company was a huge influence on Wall Street, and its revenues were in the billions.

"Hannah, your father is a very wealthy man." He couldn't quite keep the dismay out of his voice. "Obviously, you aren't in need of money. Some of the bills in this envelope are practically brand-new, so the money couldn't have been in the display cabinet when you bought it three years ago."

Hannah pulled her hands free of his. "You think somebody planted the money in that cabinet."

Ransom frowned. "You think the same thing."

Picking up her fork, she pushed her salad around on her plate, not looking at him. "I have a suspicion, that's all. I think it was Sully—the cop. He either planted it to make it look like I was taking money for illicit purposes, or…"

"Or what?"

"Or he hid it there, hoping to come back later and get it."

They were both silent for a moment. For Ransom, everything clicked neatly into place. Now he knew who the men were that he'd seen earlier, and he knew what they wanted, and the knowledge chilled him.

Hannah raised her head. "What do we do?"

What do we *do*. Like they were already partners. Something in Ransom's chest tightened. "I won't let anything happen to you."

She gave him such a look of utter trust that Ransom's chest tightened. Again he wanted to haul her across the table and keep her safe within the protective circle of his arms.

"Are you going to eat that salad, or just push it around?" His voice was gruff.

Hannah laid her fork down. "I guess I'm not that hungry."

"Then let's get out of here." He pushed both envelopes across the table to her. "As far as I'm concerned, these belong to you. Do what you want with them."

Hannah picked up the dossier. "I'm not thrilled that you did a background check on me," she said carefully, "but I think I understand your motives. And I just want to thank you for not reading the file. It means a lot to me. As for this—" She pushed the money back toward him with a distasteful grimace. "I don't want it. Turn it over to the police or make a charitable donation, but get rid of it."

Ransom tucked the envelope under his arm and smiled ruefully. "I don't deserve your understanding. In fact, I feel I should make it up to you somehow." He leaned forward and dropped his voice an octave, letting his gaze drift over her lips and lower, to where her sundress plunged downward and revealed the gentle swell of her breasts. "I can think of several ways I'd like to start."

Hannah didn't answer, but the smile she gave him was full of promise.

WHEN THEY LEFT the café ten minutes later, Hannah had the folder tucked firmly into her shoulder bag.

"We'll come back another time," Ransom had promised her, "when we're less preoccupied."

He hadn't been able to stop thinking about the men in the two cars, and he inwardly kicked himself for handing the file over to Hannah so readily. There might have been important information in there.

Damn.

He should have at least asked to look at the dossier after he'd given it to Hannah. But he knew that his noble gesture would have lost its meaning if he had.

She'd think he didn't trust her.

He felt the beginnings of a headache building behind his eyes, and swore silently. The last thing he needed right now was to be incapacitated by a migraine.

He'd told Hannah that he wasn't an intuitive person, but his instincts told him the presence of the two cars parked on their street wasn't happenstance. He felt—no, he *knew*—they were somehow connected to Hannah. Her father was an important man. Maybe the men worked for him.

But his gut told him that wasn't the case. He knew who the men were, and he could guess why they'd come. They wanted the money that even now was tucked inside his camo jacket. His lips tightened. They were in for a big disappointment.

Ransom handed Hannah into the front seat, and pulled slowly away from the curb. As he was preparing to turn off the coastal road and onto the main street, he glanced into his rearview mirror and watched as a car pulled onto the street behind him.

He was too far away to be certain, but it looked a lot like the car with the three men inside. He looked at Hannah, but she seemed unaware that anything was amiss.

"Listen," he began, "I'd like you to do me a favor."

"Okay."

"I want you to sleep at my place tonight."

She swiveled her head to look at him, and a smile curved her lips. "That's not a favor, Ransom. A favor suggests a goodwill gesture, and if I agreed to spend the night with you, it would be for purely selfish reasons."

The images that rose in his mind were so vivid and so erotic that heat lashed through his midsection and settled firmly in his groin.

Oh, yeah. He wanted her again, but there were some things he needed to take care of first.

"Darlin'," he said, slanting her a meaningful look, "there's nothing I'd like more than to see you acting *selfish* in my bed. But I have some business I need to take care of on base. I'm not sure what time I'll be back, but I'll try to make it quick."

She frowned. "Okay. So…just knock on my door when you get back."

Ransom checked his rearview mirror. The car still followed them, albeit at a distance. But it wasn't so far away that he couldn't make out the silhouettes of three people inside.

He dragged his eyes away from the reflection in the mirror. "Actually, I don't just want you to sleep at my place tonight. I want you to get whatever you need from your apartment, and then I want you to go upstairs and hang out at my place."

She tilted her head in confusion. "Why?"

Ransom gave her a tolerant look. "C'mon, darling, just trust me on this. I know I haven't given you much reason to trust me, and I wouldn't blame you if you said no, but this is really, *really* important."

Hannah chewed her lip as she considered him for a moment. Finally, to his immense relief, she gave a nod. "Okay," she said quietly. "You're scaring me a little, but the thing is...I do trust you."

Ransom pulled the Land Rover to a stop in front of the apartment building and turned to look at her. "Thanks," he said quietly.

The dull throbbing behind his eyes had increased, and he knew it wouldn't be long before it became sheer misery.

"You look tired," she said softly.

Then, before he could stop her, she reached out and laid a hand along his cheek, only to jerk it back, wide-eyed.

"Ransom."

"Sorry," he muttered. "I didn't want you to know, didn't want to have to ask you for a treatment, not when..."

He didn't finish his sentence.

"Let me touch you," she said. "And no arguments."

Scooting over on the seat, she held out her hands and waited expectantly for him to move toward her. Ransom glanced into his side mirror. The car was no longer in sight, but he suspected it wasn't far away, probably pulled along the curb farther down the road. He could almost feel the unseen eyes that watched them.

He didn't object when Hannah put her hands on either side of his face and thrust her fingers into his hair to massage his scalp. She was so close that he could smell the clean, citrus fragrance of her hair, see the almost invisible pores of her smooth skin and feel the warmth of her breath against his neck. Her pupils were hugely dilated, nearly drowning out the clear blue of her irises.

He closed his eyes.

Jesus. He was in serious trouble here. He was so completely tuned into this girl that he could almost hear the individual beats of her heart. With her fingers soothing his temples and her scent surrounding him, he felt completely content for the first time he could ever recall.

He sighed in relief as the pain ebbed and became an almost undetectable twinge.

"Thanks," he murmured, and opened his eyes to see Hannah staring at him, as if she would memorize each feature.

The expression on her face mesmerized him. Soft sunlight slanted in through the windshield, gilding her skin and turning her hair to a blaze of gold. Her eyes were such a pure, clear shade of blue that he thought he could willingly fall into their depths.

"Ransom," she breathed, and leaned into him.

With a groan of surrender, he dragged her into his arms, one arm going around her while his free hand slid beneath the soft fall of her hair to cradle her scalp in his hand, before he bent his head and moved his mouth across hers.

She tasted like the raspberry iced tea she'd had at the café, and the sensation of her soft lips, combined with the small, needy sounds she made at the back of her throat, nearly did him in.

He dragged his mouth from hers and smoothed her hair back from her face. Her eyes were hazy with pleasure, her mouth soft and moist. He needed to stay focused, and with her sensual expression and eager body, Hannah was close to derailing his good intentions.

"Listen to me, darlin'," he said, and shifted so that he could unfasten a key from the ring that dangled in the ignition. "I'm going to walk you up to my apartment, and then I want you to stay there until I get back, okay?"

"I could do some work in the shop—"

"No."

She drew back a little and stared at him, eyes wide. "Jeez. Fine…nobody has ever had to force me to take a day off."

"C'mon," he said gruffly, "I'll walk you up. And I'll give you my cell phone number in case you need to reach me."

He held the door open for her, his eyes searching the length of the street as she climbed out of the Range Rover.

"What's going on?" she asked, her voice low. "You're starting to scare me. Does this have anything to do with the money?"

He slid an arm around her shoulders as they walked up to the house. "No," he fibbed. "There've been some break-ins in town, and I have a security system in my apartment." He kept his tone easy and relaxed. "You'll be fine. Mike Howard keeps an eye on the house, so it's not like anyone is going to try anything."

She pulled him to a stop on the steps that led into the hallway. "Mike Howard? You're kidding, right? Like that's supposed to make me feel better. I don't think he's going to be much of a deterrent to anyone."

Ransom arched an eyebrow. "If there's one thing the military has taught me, it's never to underestimate people."

HANNAH HADN'T BEEN inside Ransom's apartment since the first night they'd met, and she scarcely recalled what it looked like.

He closed the door behind them, and Hannah set her small overnight bag down on the floor as she looked around. The apartment was almost Spartan, and immaculately neat. He had a minimal amount of furniture, although what he did have was solid and comfortable.

"Make yourself at home," he called over his shoulder. "I'm just going to grab what I need, then head out."

The prospect of being alone in Ransom's apartment wasn't nearly as disconcerting as it should have been. She felt a strange sense of satisfaction that he trusted her enough to let her stay here without him.

She wandered into the living room, looking at the things that made this space home for him. The room was definitely masculine, with dark colors and few decorative touches. It was casual, with a sofa and a couple of deep easy chairs, and a big-screen television up against one wall. She could picture him lounging on the sofa, feet up on the arm, watching a football game, a beer cradled in one hand.

On the computer table by the window, there were several framed photos, and she picked one up to study it. It was a picture of Ransom and three other men, dressed in full combat gear, standing in a rugged mountainous region that might have been Afghanistan. It certainly didn't look like any place in the States. They carried enormous rucksacks, and the equipment that was secured to their thick vests, or strapped around their legs, had to have weighed a ton.

Tilting the picture toward the light, she studied Ransom's face. Even wearing a helmet, she could see the photo had been taken before his injury. He was squinting against the sun, and he carried some sort of machine gun in his hand that looked like it had come straight out of a Bruce Willis action movie. It was like looking at a photo of a stranger. This wasn't the Ransom Bennett she knew.

He looked tough. Scary tough.

She replaced the photo with a shiver.

There was also a portrait of a little girl who looked so much like Ransom that Hannah's heart contracted. Picking it up, she examined the child's blue eyes and dark hair. She couldn't be more than three. His little niece, she realized, and set the picture back on the table.

His kitchen was utilitarian, with pots and pans hanging over the island, and yesterday's dishes still in the sink. Wandering down the hall, she paused in the doorway to his bedroom. His bed was enormous, an acre-wide expanse of mattress heaped with pillows, and a single duvet, neatly made up. It made her own bed look small by comparison, and her imagination surged as she thought of all the things they could do on a bed that size.

Even in here, the room was tidy and the furniture minimal. A long, low dresser stood against one wall, and stacked on top of it were neat piles of black or tan T-shirts, freshly laundered, folded and sealed in plastic.

Ransom was on the far side of the room, kneeling in the open door of his closet as he shoved items into a black duffel bag. He stood up as she came to stand beside him, and hefted the duffel bag over one shoulder.

"So, uh, feel free to go to bed if you get tired."

Hannah smiled. "I'm not sure I could fall asleep in this big bed all by myself."

"Yeah, well, I'll be back as soon as I can." He put a hand on the back of her head and drew her forward so he could press a kiss against her forehead. "Get some sleep now, while you have the chance."

The husky promise in his words gave her a little thrill. "Hmm, maybe I'll wait up for you."

"I'd like that. I'll try to call you later. You can tell me what you're doing, all alone in my bed. I'd love to hear you describe it, in detail."

Hannah barely stifled a surprised laugh. "Ransom, that's naughty."

He grinned, unrepentant. "You bet. Help yourself to anything you want, okay?"

"Okay."

He held out a small slip of paper. "I've written down the code for the security system, in case you need to turn it off for any reason. Just don't forget to reactivate it. Here's my cell phone number, and Mike Howard's number. Feel free to call either of us, for any reason."

Oh, right. With a nickname like Howard the Coward, he wasn't exactly at the top of her hero-to-the-rescue list.

He pressed the paper into her hand.

"I'll see you later."

Hannah hugged her arms around her middle as she followed him back into the living room. He opened the door to the hallway, and then paused for a moment to look back at her. "Reset the security system after I leave. Keep the door locked."

She nodded, and then he was gone.

She had no idea what was going on, or why he wanted her to remain locked in his apartment, but guessed it had nothing to do with local break-ins, as he'd claimed. She'd had a sense of foreboding since she'd first entered the shop that morning and overhead his discussion with Alec.

Sighing, she wandered back down the hallway to Ransom's bedroom and flung herself onto her back across his bed. What was she going to do for an entire afternoon and evening? Rolling onto her side, she grabbed his pillow and buried her face in it. His scent still clung to the cotton casing, and if she kept her eyes closed, she could almost imagine he was there with her.

Pushing herself to a sitting position, she surveyed the room. A tall mirror over the dresser had several small photos stuck into the frame. Curious, she stood up and bent over the dresser to get a better look.

They were more military photos, mostly of Ransom with other soldiers, in battle gear. One photo, in particular, caught her attention, and she pulled it free from the mirror to inspect it more closely. It was a photo of two men dressed entirely in black, like SWAT officers she'd seen in the movies. They wore some kind of black jumpsuit, with full-body armor and helmets, night-vision goggles, gloves and gun holsters on their hips and strapped to their thighs. Each of them carried what looked like submachine guns, and they had taken up an attack stance along the wall of a building.

One of the men wore a black ski mask beneath his goggles, but the other didn't, and Hannah's breath caught as she recognized Ransom. There was no mistaking that square jaw or the thrust of broad shoulders.

She replaced the photo and turned to leave, but her attention was caught by a dark green dress uniform hanging on the back of the closet door. It was protected beneath a clear, plastic cover that couldn't hide the shiny, gold buttons that marched down the front of the jacket.

Intrigued, Hannah stepped closer, pressing the plastic against the uniform in order to see it better.

Holy cow, the entire right breast of the jacket was an explosion of color. As she peered closer, she realized it was a series of tiny ribbons, row after row of them. She counted seventeen in all.

What had Ransom done to earn so many of them?

On the left breast of the jacket, she saw his name plate in shiny black and, beneath that, some seriously important-looking medals. Patches covered one sleeve, and she smoothed the plastic over them to get a better look. There was a red patch in the shape of an arrowhead, with a dagger in the center, its sharp blade extended upward, and above it, the word *Airborne*.

She was still admiring the patches and ribbons when someone knocked on the apartment door, causing her to jump guiltily and then freeze.

What had Ransom said?

Keep the door locked. Don't go down to the shop.

Had he told her not to open the door?

She couldn't remember.

Creeping into the living room, she tiptoed over to the door and placed her eye against the peephole.

With a groan, she deactivated the security system, flipped the deadlock back and swung the door open.

14

"WHAT ARE YOU DOING HERE?" she asked in bewilderment.

Mike Howard blinked at her through the thick lenses of his glasses before glancing furtively down the staircase that led to Hannah's apartment.

"I, um, got a call from Chief Bennett," he said, and his gaze slid over her, missing nothing, before shifting quickly away again.

"Is everything okay?"

"Yes, Chief Bennett just wanted me to check on you and let you know that I'm right next door if you need me. Right next door."

When he spoke, the words came out in a rush, slurring together in his haste to get them out. His voice was so earnest, and his expression so sincere, that Hannah couldn't help but smile at him.

"Thank you, Mr. Howard. That's very sweet of you." She stepped back and opened the door wider. "Do you want to come in? I'm not sure what Ransom has in the way of drinks but I could probably find something."

Howard took a hasty step backward and his face expressed his dismay. "Oh, no! No, no. I won't come in. I just wanted to check on you, like I promised I'd do."

"What's the matter?" Hannah asked sweetly. "Did you lose your binoculars?"

His pale face flushed. "I keep an eye on my neighbors," he said defensively. "Never know when something might happen."

"Ah. And that includes digging through their trash?"

"You can find out a lot about a person from their trash. That's how I found about your—about what happened to you in Boston. I saw it in that newspaper you threw away."

Hannah stared at him. "The newspaper you gave to the reporter?" she asked, when she found her voice.

"He came back. He was looking for you but you were gone."

Hannah frowned. "The reporter was here?"

Mike nodded, but he wouldn't meet her eyes, glancing around her instead and shifting his weight from foot to foot. "Yes. He said he wanted to talk to you about what happened in Boston."

Hannah felt the color drain from her face. "He told you what?"

Mike took another step back. "Said he wanted to talk to you about—"

Hannah put out a hand to stop him. "I heard you."

Hot waves of panic washed over her. She told herself it was inevitable that people would find out what she'd been through in Boston; she just hadn't thought it would be so soon. She wasn't ready to talk to a reporter about those days, but if she didn't, then he might run a story without having all the facts. That could spell disaster for her fledgling business.

"Did he say anything else?"

"No, no. Not to me."

Mike was already backing up, crossing and uncrossing his arms in his discomfort. His gaze skittered almost desperately toward the staircase. In another minute, he'd be gone.

"Mike, you were in the military, right?"

To Hannah's amazement, Mike's demeanor changed. He straightened his shoulders and puffed out his chest, and for the first time, met her gaze directly. "Yes, ma'am. First Battalion, 28th Infantry."

Hannah nodded as if she actually understood what that meant. "So you would recognize a patch if you saw one?"

A frown flickered across his face. "A patch?"

"Maybe that's not the right word. Maybe it's an insignia." She put out a hand to keep him from running off. "Wait right here."

Without waiting to see if he did as she asked, she ran back to Ransom's bedroom and took his uniform down from the closet door. Holding it carefully, she carried it back into the living room.

"See this patch, here?" She held up the uniform for his inspection, showing him the red arrowhead patch on the sleeve. "Ransom told me he was Special Forces. Do you know what this patch represents? Is he like a Green Beret?"

Mike blanched when he saw the red patch, and glanced swiftly around, as if he expected Ransom to materialize from the woodwork. "Army Ranger," he muttered.

"He's an Army Ranger?"

"*Was* an Army Ranger."

Hannah chewed her lip. "So what is he now?"

"Can't say. Code of silence."

What? Hannah was aware of the first stirrings of dread.

"What do you mean, a code of silence?"

Casting a furtive peek down the staircase, Mike leaned forward. His eyes had bugged behind the thick lenses of his glasses, and his expression was tight. His voice, when he finally spoke, was no more than a hiss of breath.

"Delta Force."

Then he was gone, rabbiting down the staircase and out the front door of the building before Hannah could ask him anything more.

Hannah closed the door and flipped the dead bolt, and stood still for a moment. Then she headed to the living room and Ransom's computer. Forty minutes of Internet research later, she carefully returned the uniform to the hook behind the closet door. On her way out of the bedroom, she paused to look at the photograph on the mirror. Now she understood the black jumpsuits and night-vision goggles.

Delta Force, a covert military group so secret that even the government refused to publicly acknowledge its existence. The men recruited for its elite ranks were trained killers.

She shivered. So much made sense to her now, including why Ransom wouldn't talk about his military experiences, or how he'd been injured, and why he was able to conduct such a thorough background check on her in such a short amount of time.

Why he was so distrustful.

But she couldn't reconcile the man she knew—rough and crude, yet gentle and considerate—with the men who wore the Delta insignia. She'd read they were ruthless and completely lacking in emotion.

That description didn't fit Ransom.

He was the most passionate man she knew.

The decisions he made might be based on facts, rather than emotion, but there was no denying he was capable of deep feelings.

Maybe, even, for her.

THE SOUND OF BREAKING glass woke Hannah from a restless sleep. Pushing her hair back from her face, she rose on one elbow, disoriented, and it was several long seconds before she realized where she was.

In Ransom's bed.

Alone.

After a long afternoon and evening, with no word from Ransom, she'd finally given up waiting and had gone into his room to sleep. There was a part of her that had been tempted to return to her own apartment, but discovering Ransom was part of Delta Force made her reconsider. He wouldn't have wanted her to stay in his apartment without a valid reason.

She trusted him on this.

The air conditioner in the window emitted a low, vibrating hum, making it difficult to hear anything else. Had she imagined the noise? Peering at the bedside clock, she saw it was just after two in the morning.

Where was Ransom?

There it was again, the tinkle of broken glass, muted but distinct. With a frown, Hannah threw back the covers, crept over to the air conditioner and flipped it off. It died with a soft whirr, and she stood for a moment, listening. The apartment was eerily silent.

Frowning, she turned to switch on a light, when she heard the unmistakable sound of something heavy being knocked over in the rooms beneath Ransom's apartment. Her shop and her apartment were the only rooms on the first floor of the building.

She stopped breathing, and her heart began to knock hard against her ribs. *Someone was in her shop.*

For a moment, she was too terrified to move. Her South Boston shop had been vandalized, and the experience had left her feeling violated and afraid. She'd been so grateful when Officer Sullivan had come around often to check on her. She just hadn't realized that she had more to fear from him than any burglar.

But she'd never had to confront an intruder, and didn't think she'd have the courage to do so now. But Ransom had a security system for his apartment. Whoever was downstairs couldn't gain access to his apartment without activating the alarm. The police would arrive within minutes. The thought gave her courage, even as a niggling doubt crept into her mind. Had she reset the alarm after Mike had left? She couldn't remember.

Creeping over to one of the bedroom windows, she gingerly pushed aside the curtain and peered out at the street, and then down at the walkway leading to the front door. The streetlights directly in front of the house weren't working, and the entire area was pitch-black. It was so dark, she couldn't see anything.

A heavy thunk came from somewhere directly beneath her, and Hannah froze. She couldn't tell if the disturbance had come from the shop or her apartment.

She needed to call Ransom. Or the police.

Tiptoeing into the living room, she tried to recall where she'd left her purse, with her cell phone inside. On the couch? Or by the door? She was groping her hands along the cushions of the sofa when she heard footsteps on the staircase outside Ransom's apartment.

She jerked upright and nearly stopped breathing.

It wasn't Ransom.

The footsteps were stealthy, and as the stair treads creaked, Hannah realized there was more than one person creeping their way furtively up the stairs. Suddenly, Ransom's security system seemed woefully inadequate.

Where the hell was her pocketbook?

She turned back to the sofa, just as a hand clamped hard over her mouth and an arm came around her waist, yanking her against an immobile chest.

Panic, hot and furious, surged through her and she lashed out with her arms and tried to tear herself free.

To her horror, she found herself lifted completely off her feet and her arms pinned to her sides as if she were no more than a rag doll.

"Shh. Hannah, it's *me*."

Ransom's voice hissed warmly in her ear, but it was a full second before his words penetrated her brain. When they did, she sagged against him in utter relief. She hadn't heard him, hadn't even sensed him behind her. How had he gotten into the apartment without her realizing it?

He supported her effortlessly, and as his arm loosened around her waist, allowing her feet to touch the ground, he drew his hand away from her mouth.

"Oh, my God," she whispered furiously, "you scared me to death!"

"Sorry," he breathed, sounding anything but apologetic. "Listen, we need to get out of here."

He turned her to face him, and in the darkness of the living room, he was nothing more than a looming mass of utter blackness. Everything about him was black, from the hat he wore, to his clothing and—holy crap—were those night-vision goggles pushed back on his forehead?

"What's happening? I heard noises, in my apartment and outside, in the hallway." Her voice sounded frightened, even to her own ears.

"Yeah, there are some very bad characters trying to break in," he whispered, as a subtle noise sounded just outside the door to Ransom's apartment.

As noises went, it wasn't much, but the furtiveness of it caused the hair on Hannah's neck to stand up.

"Come on," Ransom said, taking her hand. "Let's get you out of here."

They moved through the kitchen toward the balcony, and it wasn't until Hannah felt a warm blast of humid heat that she realized the sliding doors were wide open.

Ransom drew her quickly outside and before Hannah could protest, picked her up in his arms. She heard his swift, indrawn breath. "*Jesus.* What are you wearing?"

Not much.

"A T-shirt and panties."

His voice was strangled. "Don't you own a pair of pajamas?"

"I wasn't exactly expecting to be evacuated from your apartment in the middle of the night," she hissed back. "I actually expected—"

She didn't finish the thought. Didn't want him to know that she'd been expecting him to come home and join her in that big bed.

He gave a soft groan before pressing a brief, hard kiss to her lips. Hannah would have clung to him, but he was already lifting her over the railing.

"Not a whisper," he cautioned. "Billy is going to take you from here."

Only then did Hannah realize there was a man dangling on the other side of the balcony, dressed in the same black clothing that Ransom wore. He hung upright, suspended from a series of ropes that reminded Hannah of the kind that rock climbers used.

"Put your arms around my neck, and wrap your legs around my waist," Billy instructed, his voice no more than a breath of sound.

As Ransom lifted her onto Billy's back, she did as he instructed. Something cold and hard bit the inside of her bare thigh. A weapon? Her chest tightened with dread. As she wrapped her arms around his neck, she could feel the steely plates of body armor that protected his torso.

From behind them, there came a crashing noise, as if somebody was breaking their way through the door to Ransom's apartment.

Hannah's arms tightened convulsively around Billy's neck, and she cast a frantic look toward Ransom.

He didn't say a word, just pointed two fingers at Billy in a gesture that said, *Go*.

Billy released a safety catch on the rope, and they glided silently downward until his feet were on the ground. Without giving Hannah time to react, he stepped back into the shadow of the house and allowed her to slide from his back. With one deft movement, he released the rope from where it was anchored to the second-floor balcony, and it fell in a snakelike mass at his feet. Billy coiled it swiftly, then clipped it to his waist.

"I'm going to take you to Mike Howard's house," he breathed into Hannah's ear. "No talking until then, okay?"

Hannah nodded mutely, and Billy put his arm around her shoulders, pulling her into the protective bulk of his body. The backyard was small, but Hannah had never felt so exposed as they made their way across the property to the line of shrubbery that separated her yard from Mike Howard's. Beneath her bare feet, the thick grass was slick with dew.

Drawing her to a halt beneath an overhanging pine, Billy pushed her up against the rough trunk, shielding her body with his own as he surveyed their surroundings. Hannah twisted her face and looked back toward Ransom's apartment. The night was black and utterly silent, but she thought she glimpsed several dark shadows along the paler clapboards of the house. Shadows that *moved*.

She must have made a noise, because Billy put a finger over her mouth, and his eyes warned her into silence. After a moment, he nodded at her and Hannah intuitively understood they needed to move again.

Keeping close to his side, they made their way to Mike Howard's driveway, using his car as cover. The gravel bit into her feet, but with Billy pulling her relentlessly alongside, there was no time to protest or step gingerly. They reached Mike's back door, but Billy didn't knock. Instead, he withdrew a small tool from a pocket on his vest, and with two deft twists, unlocked the door and slipped inside, pulling Hannah with him.

Only when they were inside the house did Billy speak.

"Are you okay?"

She nodded, aware that she was breathing hard in a way that had nothing to do with their sprint across the yard. She was terrified.

"What's going on?" she gasped. "I saw men back there, and someone was trying to break into Ransom's apartment and, omigod, what if they have *guns?*"

Billy put his hands on her shoulders and began briskly rubbing her upper arms, as if to warm her. "The men you saw are ours, and Ransom can take care of himself," he assured her. "Listen, you're hyperventilating." He pushed her into a sitting position on the floor and with a hand at the back of her head, forced her to lean forward. "Breathe," he commanded.

Hannah did, and slowly some of the panic subsided. She lifted her head to find Billy crouched beside her, watching her intently. Even in the darkness of Mike Howard's hallway, his gray eyes glittered.

"Thanks," she said, when she could. "I didn't realize my breathing…"

Billy grinned. "Sweetheart," he drawled, "ain't nobody but me and your old man ever heard you breathe like *that*."

Her old man. As in Ransom.

Before she could respond, he rose to his feet in a swift, silent movement that was startling to watch. In the next instant, Hannah saw he held a man pinned against the wall with one forearm across the man's throat.

"No, wait!" Hannah pushed herself to her feet. "That's Mike Howard."

Slowly, Billy released the other man.

Mike's hands went jerkily to his neck, and his face was a pale blur in the darkness of the hallway.

"Sorry about that," Billy offered. "Hannah needs a safe place to stay," he explained to the other man. "Chief Bennett said you'd watch out for her."

Mike nodded, his gaze shifting to Hannah. "Yes. I mean, yes, *sir.* She'll be safe here."

Billy nodded. "Excellent." He turned back to Hannah. "Stay here. Don't leave this house until the police arrive and clear the area. Got it?"

"What about Ransom?" She couldn't keep her voice from wobbling.

Billy gave her a reassuring grin. "This is what he does best, ma'am. He'll be fine. Keep the lights off and remember, stay inside. And, Mike?"

"Yessir?"

"Give the lady a pair of shorts." He disappeared back into the night, and although Hannah strained to watch him through the window, he vanished, blending in completely with the dark.

Mike came to stand beside her, holding out a pair of white shorts with his face carefully averted, as if he'd only just realized she wore nothing but a T-shirt and underwear. "Here, it's all I have."

"Oh, thank you." Mike was a small man, and although the shorts hung low on her hips, at least they didn't fall off.

"So what's going on?" Mike asked. "Nobody said there'd be trouble. There hasn't ever been trouble on this street. Not until you moved in."

"What a surprise," Hannah breathed, still straining to see what was happening next door. "I'm not sure why, but I seem to attract trouble."

"Must have to do with those strangers I saw earlier," he mused darkly. "Drove by the house a dozen times."

Hannah turned from the window. "What strangers?"

"Strange men."

"Maybe they're the ones behind the recent slew of break-ins," she suggested.

Mike frowned. "There haven't been any break-ins. Who said anything about break-ins? Cliftondale hasn't had a break-in in years."

"Really?" And just like that, the truth hit her.

Sully had found her.

"Oh, my God," she breathed. Her attention snapped back to the window and to whatever nameless horrors might be occurring inside Ransom's apartment. "He has no idea what he's up against."

"What?" Mike came to stand beside her, pushing his glasses up higher on his nose as he peered through the window. "What is he up against?"

Hannah turned and looked at Mike, unable to keep the fear and worry out of her voice. "Officer Ned Sullivan, the dirty Boston cop who tried to have me convicted of a crime I didn't commit. Ransom has no idea how ruthless this man can be, and there are rumors…"

"What kind of rumors?"

"That he's involved in organized crime. That he works for Craig Cronin."

Mike blanched, and Hannah could see he'd heard of Craig Cronin. Who hadn't?

"I better get over there," he muttered.

"You can't," she said, dismayed. "You could be hurt. Besides, you said Ransom is—"

"Shh!" Mike cut her off with a slashing motion of his hand through the air. "Don't even say it! And it don't matter what he is. A brother in arms is in trouble. It's my *duty* to help."

Hannah watched as he went to the hallway closet and pulled out a black windbreaker and yanked it on, drawing the hood over his head and tying it tightly. With his thick glasses and slight frame, he could have been a geeky school kid.

"Mike," she began, "I'm not sure this is a good idea."

"I'm going," he said stubbornly, his hand on the doorknob. "I know what the kids call me. Howard the Coward. And maybe it's true, but if they'd seen the things I've seen, they'd be afraid, too!"

"Mike, wait." Without thinking, she reached out and laid a hand over his, and then snatched it back, shocked. Mike Howard was a man in pain. In the instant that she'd touched him, she'd felt the anguish and guilt and fear that consumed him; leftover remnants of the war that had destroyed his life. And in that moment, she knew she couldn't stop him from going next door.

"Be careful," she admonished softly.

And then he was gone.

Hannah stood in Mike's dark living room for endless minutes and strained her eyes to see what was happening next door. Lurid images filled her imagination, and she hugged herself tightly, praying that Ransom would be okay.

Once, she saw a thin strobe of light flickering through her first-floor apartment, but it was quickly extinguished. A few moments later she saw two shadowy figures moving through the yard, but they were gone so swiftly that she couldn't even be sure she'd seen them.

The sound of police sirens sounded in the distance, growing steadily closer as she listened. But it wasn't until four cruisers turned onto the street that relief poured through her. Everything would be okay now.

15

OPENING THE FRONT DOOR of Mike's house, Hannah ran across the driveway as the cruisers screeched to a stop in front of the shop and eight police officers emerged. Flashing blue lights sliced through the darkness, and the static squawk of a police radio interrupted the silence.

One of the police officers spotted her immediately and, before she could protest, pulled her behind the protective barrier of a cruiser.

"Ma'am, you shouldn't be out here," she said sternly. "Stay here and don't move."

"I live in that house," Hannah explained in a rush. "Someone tried to break in."

"Yes, ma'am," she said. "Your neighbor called us. Said he was going in to stop them. Now please, stay back and stay *down* until we clear the scene."

Hannah stared at the officer, dumbfounded. Mike had called the police? When? As he'd gone to retrieve a pair of shorts for her? He hadn't been gone long enough to place a phone call. The entire time she'd been in his house, he hadn't made a phone call to anyone, never mind the police.

"Are you sure—"

"Ma'am, you can make a report later, but right now you need to let us do our job." The officer's voice was brusque, and Hannah meekly nodded, watching as the police surrounded the house with their weapons drawn and then cautiously entered the building.

She waited, her nerves stretched taut, as first one light, and then another flicked on inside the house. Two more police cruisers arrived, along with several unmarked cars. Hannah was only vaguely aware that the lights were slowly coming on in the neighboring homes, as the flashing lights and strident police radios woke the nearby residents.

"Ms. Hartwell?"

Hannah turned to see a young man standing at her elbow. The blue strobe lights from the cruiser flashed across his features, but it wasn't until she saw the camera in his hands that she recognized him.

The reporter from the newspaper.

What was his name?

"Bob Carroll," he said, putting out his hand.

She took it automatically, and her eyes widened as behind him, a television van rolled to a stop alongside the curb and a camera crew jumped out.

"Uh, yes, I remember you," she said, dragging her attention back to Bob.

"I got an anonymous call that a B and E was under way at your shop," he said. "Is that true?"

He'd gotten a call?

She nodded dumbly. "Uh-huh. I mean, I think so. I wasn't home, so I'm not sure if it was my shop or my apartment that got broken into." She gestured toward the house. "The police just went in."

Bob followed her gaze. Two policemen appeared at the front door, and one of them spoke into his handheld radio, while the second gestured that the house had been secured. Standing between them was Mike Howard, looking slightly dazed.

"Excuse me," Bob said, touching her arm. "I'm going to see what's happened. Will you be available afterward? For a comment?"

Hannah nodded mutely, staring as the television crew moved toward the house, their cameras trained on the police officers and Mike.

"Excuse me, ma'am?"

Hannah turned to see another policeman by her elbow.

"I understand you're the tenant?"

"Yes. Did you catch the intruder?"

The police officer made an annotation on a notepad he carried. "Yes, ma'am, we did. We have all five perps in custody, thanks to your neighbor, Mr. Howard."

"Five?"

"Yes, ma'am. They're not talking right now, and they're not carrying any identification, but we'll sort it out soon enough. You're lucky you weren't home—these guys were armed to the teeth. Real professionals."

Oh, God. They'd taken Ransom and his buddies into custody by mistake.

"Can I— May I see them?" she asked.

How was it possible that they'd been arrested? Delta Force soldiers were supposed to be the best. The elite.

The policeman jotted something down on his notepad, and then gestured with his head toward the house. "They're being brought out now. I wouldn't recommend you go inside, however." He glanced pointedly at her bare feet. "There's a lot of broken glass and upended furniture. No major damage, but you probably want to get some footwear on before going in."

Hannah turned to look at the house, and as the television camera rolled, and Bob the reporter snapped pictures, Sully emerged from the house, escorted by two policemen.

Hannah couldn't suppress her gasp.

The police officer snapped his attention to her. "Do you know him?"

Hannah nodded mutely.

Both of Sully's eyes were swelled nearly shut, and blood

oozed from his nose, but there was no mistaking him. Hannah put a hand to her mouth and hoped his two black eyes prevented him from seeing her clearly. She watched as Mick Mahoney was led out next, followed by three more men, all of them wearing dark clothing and sullen expressions.

"You'll need to come with us to the station to make a statement," the officer said. "We may need your assistance in identifying them."

Each man was handcuffed and led to a waiting cruiser, while the television reporter thrust a microphone into their faces and fired questions at them. Bob followed closely behind, scribbling frantically on his notepad.

"Is that all of them?" she asked, when the last man had been pushed into the backseat of a police car. There was no sign of Ransom or Billy, or the other men she was now certain had been involved.

The officer gave her a wry smile. "That's all of them. Mike did some good work tonight—he had them hog-tied and gagged by the time we got here. I guess after this, they won't be calling him *Howard the Coward* anymore." He shook his head in amazement. "It still blows my mind—little Mike against five thugs. I guess he's a lot tougher than he looks."

Hannah turned to look at Mike. He was standing on the front lawn, talking to the police and gesturing wildly with his hands. Hannah could only guess what he was saying, but knew instinctively he would protect the identities of Ransom and his men.

"Yes." She smiled. "He's a good neighbor."

FROM THE CONCEALING shadows of the nearby tree line, Ransom watched with grim satisfaction as the five men were led to the police cruisers and stashed in the backseats. They deserved whatever they had coming to them, and thanks to Alec, they'd get plenty.

While conducting his background check on Hannah, Alec had also compiled a dossier on Officer Ned "Sully" Sullivan that included racketeering, extortion, tampering with evidence and conspiring to take payoffs in return for protecting some of the most notorious leaders of organized crime on the Eastern Seaboard.

Even now, one copy of the dossier was being delivered anonymously to Bob Carroll at his news office, and another one to the FBI. Ransom suspected that by early tomorrow afternoon, the FBI would launch a full-scale investigation into Sully's dirty dealings. If he was convicted on even a fraction of the crimes he'd committed, Sully would go to prison for a very long time.

Ransom watched Hannah with greedy eyes. She'd managed to find a pair of white shorts to cover her minuscule panties, but they hung low on her hips, exposing a smooth strip of bare skin beneath the hem of her T-shirt.

More than anything, he wanted to hold her.

When he thought of what Sully and his men had intended to do to her, his blood ran cold. He couldn't even think about what might have happened if he hadn't asked Alec to run a background check on Hannah, and in the process, Alec hadn't uncovered evidence of Sully's criminal activities.

Sully hadn't intended to let Hannah live.

Ransom's chest ached as he watched her. She was so damned beautiful. So full of hope. So full of love.

Maybe even for him.

Christ, he hoped so.

His cell phone vibrated silently at his hip, and moving stealthily away from the property, he pulled it out and read the text message.

CONGRATULATIONS. AM WATCHING YOUR WORK VIA CLOSED CIRCUIT. LOOKS LIKE YOU'RE FULLY RECOVERED. SINCE YOU'RE ABLE-BODIED, PLAN ON GOING WHEELS UP IN 24. COL L.

This was it, what he'd been waiting for. A thumbs-up from his commanding officer that he'd be a part of Operation *Formidable Force.*

He should have been elated.

Instead, all he could think was that he didn't want to leave the woman he loved.

HANNAH CLOSED the door of her apartment and kicked off the flip-flops that the Cliftondale police department had loaned to her—standard government-issue shower thongs, usually reserved for prisoners.

God, she was tired to her very bones. She'd never guessed from watching *Law and Order* reruns that providing a police statement could be so exhausting. Or so time-consuming.

Despite the grueling night she'd had, she still smiled when she thought of Mike Howard. The police couldn't understand how he'd managed to subdue all five men by himself, and even the perps themselves hadn't been able to explain it.

One of Sully's men had confided to the police that their capture had unfolded much like a horror film. They'd known they were being stalked through the apartment building, but they hadn't known by whom.

They'd been picked off neatly and quietly, thug by thug. First one and then another of their gang would silently vanish in the darkness, their numbers systematically reduced until only Sully had remained. Unlike the others, however, he'd endured a punishing beating before he'd been hog-tied and gagged alongside his cronies. Each of the five men claimed they'd heard nothing, nor had they seen another person until the lights came on and they'd found Mike Howard standing over them.

It was almost seven in the morning by the time a police officer dropped Hannah off at her apartment. This was usually the time when she'd be waking up, but all she could think about was going to bed. Sully and his men had overturned some of her furniture, and upended several boxes of her belongings, but Hannah was grateful no permanent damage had been done to her apartment. In her shop, they'd smashed the display cabinet in their search for the money, and had destroyed some inventory, but it could have been much worse.

She quickly washed her face and brushed her teeth. Then, shucking her clothing, she padded naked into her bedroom, only to stop abruptly in the doorway.

Ransom lay sprawled on top of her bed wearing nothing but a pair of boxer shorts and, beneath them, a very impressive erection. As he raked his gaze over her body, the heat in his eyes nearly incinerated her on the spot.

Hannah didn't hesitate, but launched herself at him, covering his body with her own and relishing the feel of him beneath her hands. She wanted to touch him everywhere, to feel his body sliding against hers.

He laughed, and caught her face in both hands and kissed her hungrily.

Urgently.

Their lips fused in a soul-sucking kiss that made Hannah moan and seek more contact with the hard flesh pressed against her center.

When Ransom finally released her, she bent to press heated kisses along his neck and collarbone, and lower. She grazed her teeth over his nipples, while her hands reached between them and gripped him through the thin fabric of his boxers.

"I was so scared for you," she gasped between kisses, loving how he arched beneath her, loving how readily he responded to her touch.

Loving him.

"I know, darlin'," he said roughly, tangling his hands in her hair as she skated her mouth across his stomach. "I wanted to let you know I was okay, but— *Christ.*"

His strangled voice made Hannah look up from her task and shoot him a seductive smile.

"What's the matter?" she asked sweetly. "You can give it but you can't take it?" She breathed warmly against his rigid arousal through the boxers, before sucking him gently into her mouth, fabric and all.

"I can give it *and* take it," he growled, and before Hannah could guess his intent, he pulled her up and turned her beneath him. His eyes glittered hotly as he took in her flushed features. "Anytime, anywhere."

"Then how about right now?" she breathed and, reaching up, slanted her mouth across his, mating her tongue with his and wanting to devour him; to pull him completely inside her and keep him safe.

"Ah, darlin'," he rasped, "you feel so damned good." His hands trembled as they cupped her breasts. He stroked his thumbs across her nipples until they beaded into hard peaks, and then slid his fingers down the length of her body to cup her buttocks and press her hips against his. His breathing was ragged, his hands demanding.

"I want you now," she panted against his lips, and lifting her legs, wrapped them around his waist, rubbing herself sinuously against his erection. "Now, now…"

Reaching down between their straining bodies, he found her wet and ready for him. He eased a finger into her, and then another, and she writhed against him, moaning and crying her need.

Raising himself away from her, Ransom shoved his boxers down, and Hannah helped him, using her feet to push them completely free. With his eyes fastened on her, he spread her knees and positioned himself at the entrance to her body.

Hannah felt her insides tremble. Her hands were unsteady as they traveled over his shoulders and down the rock-hard muscles of his arms.

He grimaced as he eased himself a scant inch inside. "Ah… you're so tight."

She wanted him. All of him. Arching her hips, she tried to urge him in farther, but he grasped her hands and pushed them over her head and held them there. He stared down at her, his blue eyes shimmering in the semidarkness of the bedroom.

"Do you trust me?" he breathed.

"Yes," she managed, and hooked one foot across his back, trying to bring him closer.

He slid in another inch, drawing a small gasp of pleasure from her.

"I have to leave tomorrow," he said tightly, holding her gaze. "I don't know how long I'll be gone."

Oh, God. She'd known this day was going to come, but it was too soon. She wasn't ready.

Her face must have mirrored her distress, because he bent his head and kissed her so sweetly that she began to cry.

"Please come back to me," she begged, drawing in ragged breaths. "Please…"

"Do you love me?" The question was a soft growl, and evading it wasn't an option.

"Yes," she gasped. "Oh, yes."

He thrust himself all the way home, keeping his eyes on hers, and Hannah felt herself breaking apart at the expression on his face.

Everything he felt for her was there in his eyes. There might be things he'd never be able to share with her, but this wasn't one of them. Slowly, he withdrew his body from hers, and then sank back into her, stroking her intimately and creating a friction that made her pulse with need.

He released her hands, and she clung to him as he moved hard and deep inside her, his face scant inches from her own, his eyes locked with hers. Hannah felt the full force of his love and need and desperation for her, and it took her breath away. She'd never felt such an emotional connection with anyone before.

"Say it," he demanded raggedly, and Hannah knew he was close to losing control. "I need to hear you say it."

She arched against him, loving how he stroked inside her, long and hot and deep. An orgasm was building, and when he cupped her buttocks and slid a finger between them to touch her more intimately than anyone ever had, she felt herself shatter completely.

"I love you," she cried.

He captured her soft sobs with his mouth, and as she splintered apart, her body fisting around his in spasms of intense pleasure, he let out a harsh cry and thrust deeply, spilling himself inside her welcoming body.

HANNAH LAY with Ransom sprawled on top of her, his breathing harsh in her ear. She stroked her hands over his back, loving how solid and warm he felt, loving how his weight pressed her into the mattress. She never wanted the moment to end; never wanted to let him go.

When he finally raised his head to look at her, his eyes were suspiciously bright. "I can't stay."

She closed her eyes, unwilling for him to see her cry, and nodded. "I understand."

"I'll come back." He cupped her face in his hands and forced her to look at him. "I will come home, Hannah."

Hannah hugged him, burying her face in his shoulder and nodding that she'd heard him. But she couldn't meet his eyes. She wanted desperately to believe him, but she knew there were some things that even a Delta Force operator couldn't control.

16

Three months later

IN THE BACK ROOM of her shop, Hannah pulled the sheet off the massage table and tossed it into the nearby hamper. Soft music drifted through the room from the wall-mounted speakers she'd had installed, and an aromatherapy candle flickered on a low stand, filling the space with the light scent of sandalwood. As always, the woodsy aroma reminded her of Ransom.

Outside, it was dark. Soft snow flurries had been falling all day, an early Christmas present for the kids of Cliftondale. Hannah walked over to the shelving units that Billy Pagan had built for her and drew a clean sheet from the folded stack, making a mental note to order some more. Even with a laundry service providing clean linens, she could barely keep up with her growing clientele. She was tired, but satisfied in a way she'd never thought she'd be.

Well, mostly satisfied.

She hadn't heard anything from Ransom in nearly six weeks, and the last communication had been no more than a brief e-mail telling her that he was okay. She didn't know where he was or how long he'd be gone. Was he getting enough to eat? Was he safe? Did his migraines bother him?

Did he think about her sometimes?

The endless worrying was beginning to take its toll on Hannah. She had dark circles beneath her eyes, and she'd lost weight. Meditation and positive self-talk only went so far in allaying her fears; she wanted *him*, at home and in her arms.

God, she missed him so much.

To keep herself from going nuts, she stayed busy. Crazy busy. She'd treated twelve clients throughout the course of the day, most of them soldiers returning from Iraq or Afghanistan. Her primary service was her Reiki treatments, but occasionally she'd get a service member whose injuries required more immediate relief.

For those special cases, she'd treat them with her own form of hands-on healing, although she'd deny it to anyone who asked. The result, however, was a constant stream of war veterans coming through her door seeking help.

Hannah was more than happy to give it.

The door to the back room opened and her good friend and assistant, Maureen Hurley, poked her head through.

"I think that's it for the day," she said, then frowned as she watched Hannah shake out the clean sheet and spread it over the massage table. "Hey, honey, you look like hell. Here, let me do that. You need to go home and soak in a long bath or something. You work too hard. And you're too thin. Didn't you eat that sandwich I brought you for lunch?"

Hannah gave her friend a tolerant look, but relinquished the sheet into Maureen's capable hands, watching as she tucked the edges in.

"Have I told you how glad I am that you decided to move down here?" she asked, although she knew she had, at least once a day.

Maureen grinned at her. "My decision had nothing to do with you. As soon as I found out the neighboring town was called *Morehead City,* I knew it was the place for me. I mean, c'mon, who wouldn't want to live in a town called More Head? Oh, yes, *please!*"

Hannah laughed.

"Speaking of which," Maureen continued, "I hear Mick's

getting out in less than a year." She swept her hands over the sheet, smoothing it across the massage table. "He never was much for the mob. I think he only did it because he was afraid if he didn't, Craig Cronin might take it out on his sister. He's agreed to testify against Sully and Cronin in return for an early release."

"I never had a problem with Mick," Hannah said. "He was always courteous to me."

"The things that man can do with his mouth..." Maureen sighed dramatically.

Hannah didn't like to think about Sully or the others. As far as she was concerned, Sully had already occupied far too much time in her life. She was through being afraid of him.

After he'd been arrested on charges of breaking and entering with deadly intent, Sully had also been indicted for racketeering and obstruction of justice. He had yet to go to trial, but he remained in prison pending his court date, and Hannah had it on good authority that he wouldn't be getting out anytime soon.

The bells over the front door tinkled, and Maureen scooted out of the room. "Probably just Mike," she called over her shoulder, "wanting to see how your day went."

Since the night when Sully had been arrested, Mike Howard had become something of a local celebrity. Bob Carroll had written an article about him that had made the front page of the local paper. He'd been touted as a hero by the town officials, had been recognized by the local law enforcement community as an honorary detective, and had even had a day named in his honor. Nobody called him Howard the Coward anymore.

An anonymous donation of twenty-five thousand dollars had also been made to a local veterans' hospital. Although there was much speculation in town that Mike was the donor, Hannah finally knew what Ransom had done with Sully's ill-gotten money.

In recent weeks, Mike had made a point of stopping by the shop at the end of each day to share a cup of tea with Hannah and Maureen before they closed up for the night. As Hannah moved to switch off the stereo and extinguish the candle, Maureen poked her head back through the door.

"Oh, man," she said in a whisper, "there's another soldier out here wanting a treatment. I told him we're closing up and that you're completely wiped out, but he said he's come a long way…" Maureen broke off uncertainly. "Do you want me to schedule him for tomorrow morning?"

Hannah had never turned anyone away from her shop, and she wasn't about to start now. The last thing she needed was some kind of Karmic smack-down.

"No, I'm okay," she said with an encouraging smile. "Send him on in, and then you head home. It's snowing and I hate to think of you on the roads if it gets any worse. I'll be fine."

Maureen nodded and ducked back out of the room. Hannah smoothed her hands over her hair and strove for a serene, confident demeanor. The music in the stereo came to an end, and she walked over to the shelves to choose another selection, something soothing and uplifting.

The door opened behind her.

"I'll be right with you," she said, running her finger along the selection of CDs, and finally settling on a Kitaro assortment. "Make yourself comfortable."

"Do you think it's safe for you to be back here, alone with a client?" The voice was low, almost gruff.

Hannah's heart nearly stopped.

She turned slowly, her hands braced on the shelves behind her, scarcely daring to believe it might be true. He stood just inside the doorway, and Hannah had never seen anything as wonderful or beautiful as the sight of Ransom Bennett standing in her shop.

He wore a pair of black cargo pants and boots, paired with a heavy sweater. His hair was longer, curling against his neck, and his face was deeply tanned, making the scar on his forehead stand out in stark contrast. He was leaner than she remembered. Harder. Even from across the room, Hannah could see the lines of fatigue etched around his mouth and eyes.

Her throat felt thick, and there was a peculiar burning sensation behind her eyes.

He was home.

Hannah gave him a tremulous smile. "Why wouldn't it be safe?"

He crossed the room in several long strides, until he stood directly in front of her, until only inches separated them. His dark blue eyes were suspiciously bright as they drifted over her features, lingering on each one as if he'd commit them to memory. When he spoke, his voice was husky.

"What if you get a male client who expects…more?"

Hannah's heart beat so fast she thought it might explode in her chest. "More *what?*"

"More…*everything.*"

Then she was in his arms, crushed against his chest as he buried his face in her neck and wrapped her completely in his strength and warmth, lifting her off her feet and reminding her how amazing it felt to be pressed against all that masculine hardness.

God, she'd missed him!

He smelled like the cold outdoors, and damp wool, and pure, unadulterated male.

Hannah wound her arms around his neck and clung for all she was worth, aware that he was murmuring words against her neck. Words like…*missed you…thought of you…*

Love you.

Pulling back, Ransom cupped her face in his hands and searched her eyes, before slanting his mouth across hers in a kiss that was both reverent and demanding.

When they finally pulled apart they were both gasping for air. He tipped his forehead to hers. "I thought of you every day that I was gone," he breathed. "I missed you so much."

"Me, too."

"I don't know how long I'll be home this time."

"As long as you spend that time with me…"

"Every minute," he promised. "As long as you're there for me when I come back."

"Always," she whispered fiercely. "I'll always wait for you."

"I'll always come back to you." The words were a promise.

"Did your mission…go well? How are your headaches?"

He grinned then. "Darlin', anytime I make it home alive, the mission was a success. As for the headaches, I still get them. But they're manageable. Definitely manageable."

Looking into her eyes, shimmering with love and relief, Ransom knew it was no less than the truth. Operation *Formidable Force* had been an unmitigated success. They'd found and extricated the two Delta operators who'd been held hostage. The men were a little worse for wear, but they'd pull through.

And they'd found Abdul Alkazar. Ransom's plan had been to kill the warlord, until he'd learned the reason the tribal leader had betrayed him. The Taliban had taken three of his young children and threatened to kill them unless Alkazar cooperated with them. In the end, they'd left him alive, and Ransom knew the warlord's loyalty had been swayed unerringly in their favor that day.

Ransom swept his gaze around the small room, noting the changes that had taken place in his absence. The room was a warm and vibrant reflection of Hannah's personality.

"I think your assistant left for the night," he murmured, and looked meaningfully at the massage table with its crisp, white linens.

"Ransom," Hannah said in choked voice, but he didn't miss how her eyes took on a hazy, sensual expression. "I know what you're thinking, but that mattress isn't big enough for both of us."

"Darlin'," he drawled, his voice laced with promise, "for what I have in mind, you'll be the only one spread across that bed."

"Oh," she murmured, her imagination conjuring up luscious images of what he might have in mind for her. "How lovely."

"You bet." He grinned and swept her into his arms. "And that's only the beginning...."

* * * * *

*Harlequin is 60 years old,
and Harlequin Blaze is celebrating!
After all, a lot can happen in 60 years,
or 60 minutes...or 60 seconds!
Find out what's going down in
Blaze's heart-stopping new miniseries,
FROM 0 TO 60!
Getting from "Hello" to "How was it?"
can happen fast....*

*Here's a sneak peek at the first book,
A LONG, HARD RIDE
by Alison Kent.
Available March 2009.*

"Is THAT FOR ME?" Trey asked.

Cardin Worth cocked her head to the side and considered how much better the day already seemed. "Good morning to you, too."

When she didn't hold out the second cup of coffee for him to take, he came closer. She sipped from her heavy white mug, hiding her grin and her giddy rush of nerves behind it.

But when he stopped in front of her, she made the mistake of lowering her gaze from his face to the exposed strip of his chest. It was either give him his cup of coffee or bury her nose against him and breathe in. She remembered so clearly how he smelled. How he tasted.

She gave him his coffee.

After taking a quick gulp, he smiled and said, "Good morning, Cardin. I hope the floor wasn't too hard for you."

The hardness of the floor hadn't been the problem. She shook her head. "Are you kidding? I slept like a baby, swaddled in my sleeping bag."

"In my sleeping bag, you mean."

If he wanted to get technical, yeah. "Thanks for the loaner. It made sleeping on the floor almost bearable." As had the warmth of his spooned body, she thought, then quickly changed the subject. "I saw you have a loaf of bread and some eggs. Would you like me to cook breakfast?"

He lowered his coffee mug slowly, his gaze as warm as the

sun on her shoulders, as the ceramic heating her hands. "I didn't bring you out here to wait on me."

"You didn't bring me out here at all. I volunteered to come."

"To help me get ready for the race. Not to serve me."

"It's just breakfast, Trey. And coffee." Even if last night it had been more. Even if the way he was looking at her made her want to climb back into that sleeping bag. "I work much better when my stomach's not growling. I thought it might be the same for you."

"It is, but I'll cook. You made the coffee."

"That's because I can't work at all without caffeine."

"If I'd known that, I would've put on a pot as soon as I got up."

"What time *did* you get up?" Judging by the sun's position, she swore it couldn't be any later than seven now. And, yeah, they'd agreed to start working at six.

"Maybe four?" he guessed, giving her a lazy smile.

"But it was almost two…" She let the sentence dangle, finishing the thought privately. She was quite sure he knew exactly what time they'd finally fallen asleep after he'd made love to her.

The question facing her now was where did this relationship—if you could even call it *that*—go from here?

* * * * *

Cardin and Trey are about to find out that
great sex is only the beginning….
Don't miss the fireworks!
Get ready for
A LONG, HARD RIDE
by Alison Kent.
Available March 2009,
wherever Blaze books are sold.

DIAMOND IN THE ROUGH

John Callister is a millionaire rancher, yet when he meets
lovely Sassy Peale and she thinks he's a cowboy, he goes along
with her misconception. He's had enough of gold diggers,
and this is a chance to be valued for himself, not his money.
But when Sassy finds out the truth, she feels John was merely
playing with her. John will have to convince her that he's truly
the man she fell in love with—a diamond in the rough.

THE MEN OF MEDICINE RIDGE—a brand-new miniseries
set in the wilds of Montana!

Available April 2009 wherever you buy books.

www.eHarlequin.com

HRI7577

HARLEQUIN® Romance®

This February the Harlequin® Romance series
will feature six Diamond Brides stories featuring
diamond proposals and gorgeous grooms.

Share your dream wedding proposal and you could WIN!

The most romantic entry will win a diamond
necklace and will inspire a proposal in one of
our upcoming Diamond Grooms books in 2010.

In 100 words or less, tell us the most romantic
way that you dream of being proposed to.

For more information, and to enter
the Diamond Brides Proposal contest, please visit
www.DiamondBridesProposal.com

Or mail your entry to us at:

IN THE U.S.: 3010 Walden Ave., P.O. Box 9069, Buffalo, NY 14269-9069
IN CANADA: 225 Duncan Mill Road, Don Mills, ON M3B 3K9

REQUEST YOUR FREE BOOKS!

2 FREE NOVELS
PLUS 2
FREE GIFTS!

HARLEQUIN®

Blaze™

Red-hot reads!

HB08R

HARLEQUIN® *Blaze*™

A new three book miniseries,

Stolen from Time

What's sexy now was even sexier then!

Beginning in March with

Once an Outlaw

DEBBI RAWLINS

Sam Watkins has a past he's trying to forget.
Reese Winslow is desperate to remember a way home.
Caught in the Old West, their intensely passionate affair
has them joining forces to overcome individual demons,
but will it mean they'll be together forever?

Available March 2009 wherever books are sold.

---

red-hot reads

www.eHarlequin.com

HB79459

The Inside Romance newsletter has a NEW look for the new year!

Same great content, brand-new look!

The Inside Romance newsletter is a FREE quarterly newsletter highlighting our upcoming series releases and promotions!

Click on the Inside Romance link on the front page of
www.eHarlequin.com or e-mail us at
insideromance@harlequin.ca to sign up
to receive your FREE newsletter today!

You can also subscribe by writing to us at: HARLEQUIN BOOKS
Attention: Customer Service Department
P.O. Box 9057, Buffalo, NY 14269-9057

Please allow 4-6 weeks for delivery of the first issue by mail.

IRNNEW09

You're invited to join our Tell Harlequin Reader Panel!

By joining our new reader panel you will:

- Receive Harlequin® books—they are FREE and yours to keep with no obligation to purchase anything!
- Participate in fun online surveys
- Exchange opinions and ideas with women just like you
- Have a say in our new book ideas and help us publish the best in women's fiction

In addition, you will have a chance to win great prizes and receive special gifts!
See Web site for details. Some conditions apply.
Space is limited.

To join, visit us at
www.TellHarlequin.com.

COMING NEXT MONTH
Available February 10, 2009

#453 A LONG, HARD RIDE Alison Kent
From 0–60
All Cardin Worth wants is to put her broken family together again. And if that means seducing Trey Davis, her first love, well, a girl's got to do what a girl's got to do. Only, she never expected to enjoy it quite so much....

#454 UP CLOSE AND DANGEROUSLY SEXY Karen Anders
Drew Miller's mission: train a fellow agent's twin sister to replace her in a sting op. Expect the unexpected is his mantra, but he never anticipated that his trainee, Allie Carpenter, would be teaching him a thing or twelve in the bedroom!

#455 ONCE AN OUTLAW Debbi Rawlins
Stolen from Time, Bk. 1
Sam Watkins has a past he's trying to forget. Reese Winslow is desperate to remember a way home. Caught in the Old West, they share an intensely passionate affair that has them joining forces. But does that mean they'll be together forever?

#456 STILL IRRESISTIBLE Dawn Atkins
Years ago Callie Cummings and Declan O'Neill had an unforgettable fling. And now she's back in town. He's still tempting, still irresistible, and she can't get images of him and tangled sheets out of her mind. The only solution? An unforgettable fling, round two.

#457 ALWAYS READY Joanne Rock
Uniformly Hot!
Lieutenant Damon Craig has always tried to live up to the Coast Guard motto: Always Ready. But when sexy sociologist Lacey Sutherland stumbles into a stakeout, alerting his suspects—and his libido—Damon knows he doesn't stand a chance....

#458 BODY CHECK Elle Kennedy
When sexually frustrated professor Hayden Houston meets hot hockey star Brody Croft in a bar, she's ready for a one-night stand. But can Brody convince Hayden that he's good for more than just a body check?

HBCNMBPA0209